The Mask of Emmeline Jones

MM Hurley

ISBN Printed: 979-8-9919099-0-7
ISBN Ebook:

Some sample scenarios in this book are fictitious. Any similarity to actual persons, living or dead, is coincidental.

Edited by Trista Lutgring
Cover art by Maciena Justice, Justice Designs
Cover Design and Photo Copyright © 2025 Maciena Justice

Kindle Direct Publishing

MM Hurley Imprint

MMHurley.com

Dedication

For my children, go after your dreams.

Index

Prologue

Emmeline

"While reports are still flooding in by witnesses, we know Emmeline Jones collapsed on stage while performing the first half of her setlist and was rushed to St. Catherine's Memorial Hospital. Fans are flocking there and holding a vigil outside. Right now, Erin Fisher joins us from Ronald Adams Exhibition Stadium for more details."

"Thank you, Layla," a young woman standing in front of a brightly lit stadium replied, holding a standard news microphone before her. "Witnesses are stating that during Jones's performance of her single, *The Sad Ones,* she suddenly collapsed, causing those in attendance to erupt into chaos." The on-location reporter paused for effect before continuing with her rundown of the events.

"It is speculated she went down due to a gunshot wound, though authorities are not confirming that at this time. A lock-down was placed on the stadium by staff and security to calm the panicked crowd."

The camera panned to a wider angle, showing a young woman, no more than 20, wearing a shirt with the concert's logo. "I'm here with audience member and long-time fan, Amelia Wilson. Amelia, can you tell us what you saw?"

"It was the craziest thing! We were standing there, vibing with the music, and she just stopped singing," the young fan said, biting her bottom lip. "We all knew something was off, but when she was down, her dancers formed a wall around her. The music cut out, and we could hear one of the dancers screaming for Joseph; another kept screaming Emmeline was shot. It was so scary. The whole place went into lockdown, and the lights were so bright. I've never been more scared in my whole life."

As Erin wrapped up the interview, Layla threw it to another field reporter, Hayden Barnes, who was at the hospital relaying how there were no updates but Emmeline Jones was undergoing emergency surgery for the injuries sustained on stage.

News media worldwide had jumped on my story — the CEO and founder of LJ Production Company attacked at the last concert of my most extensive tour. The details at first were sketchy. Someone had shouted, "Gunshot!" during the show and my security team quickly removed me from the arena, rushing me to the hospital. It was front-page news. Every tabloid and international publication picked up the story. Anyone who could speak my name, did so loudly. Attempting to boost their streaming numbers. While I lay naked, exposed on a surgical table, with doctors and nurses fighting to give me a chance of survival.

All because I didn't listen to my gut feeling. I knew I shouldn't have taken the stage that night, but the show must go on, as they say— the adage drove me to step out in front of the crowd, something I had done a million times.

Never before had I questioned how safe I was on stage. It was my refuge; I was strong out there. The vulnerability of my song lyrics empowered me. The cheers of the fans lifted and strengthened me. I could skip around the stage, head up, shoulders squared. I was untouchable.

The stage was a carefully choreographed flow, a certainty of who and what should be. There was no deviation from the plan on stage. But that all stopped when the hot metal penetrated my body. I couldn't catch my breath as my body betrayed me, falling backward from the momentum of the bullet striking.

Time seemed different; I wasn't sure how quickly or slowly it passed. My mind filled with blurred faces and thoughts, and I fell into a panic. It wasn't until my business partner and best friend of years, Joseph, appeared beside me that I knew everything really had happened. And his gaze told me things were as bad as they felt.

Joseph instantly jumped into action after the guards pulled me backstage. "Emme, don't leave me," he begged as he applied pressure to the wound, blood seeping from the area. I heard his sigh of relief as paramedics replaced his hands on my body.

It was at that moment I knew I had to fight. My eyes were too heavy, and I struggled to stay awake, to stay in the present. I tried to focus on whatever I could— the sounds of the panicked crowd, the heavy breathing of the dancers protecting me from the cell phones snapping photos, the voices of the paramedics and Joseph above me. But it was too much. All the noise soon faded as my eyes finally closed. Now, I could only hope those around me could save me.

Chapter One

Joseph

From the moment she left my sight, my worries amplified and pulsed through my veins.

When Emmeline was placed in the ambulance, there was no stopping me from joining her on the ride to St. Catherine's. As I followed the gurney through the hospital, I was stopped at the surgery room entrance by a nurse instructing me I could not follow.

"I have to have her back!" I yelled at the bulky man in scrubs blocking my path as we were separated by the now-closing doors.

"We'll have it now," the nurse replied calmly. He placed his hands on my shoulders, and I understood then I could no longer protect my best friend.

Now my terror for her made my mind scream in protest even more as the doctors moved further into the operating room and gathered around Emmeline.

I may have been Emme's person, but I was, first and foremost, the Chief Operating Officer of our business, LJ Productions. Even if I hated it with every fiber of my being, I would focus on that. But first, I had to get my feet to move away from the door.

"Joe," a soft, feminine voice whispered, the use of the nickname surprising me more than her appearance. "There is a lot we need to discuss."

Lydia McCaffery was the most highly sought-after media relations strategist and the love of my life. She found me with my fist curled tightly by my side, so lost in my thought I didn't even hear her approach.

"Mr. MacDonald," she stated, grabbing my attention more firmly.

"Yes," I said, a heavy sigh leaving my body as I ran my hand across my face.

"There are protocols we have set in place to handle emergencies," she said softly.

"There are," I answered, forcing my body to turn from the doors Emme had been pushed through and motioned for Lydia to lead the way.

The reporters already lining up outside the hospital made our logical next steps easier. Lydia stepped away to make all the arrangements, and somehow, I was ready to go when she returned a few minutes later.

"They are already hounding us for a statement," Lydia said, flicking her eyes down from my face to the shirt I was wearing and back. I didn't want to think about the blood stains she most likely saw there. Lydia wasn't at the venue, but she might as well have given her commitment to the job. She had already been given the play-by-play from several sources on our team and now it seemed she finally realized how bad the incident had been.

"I've also spoken to a nurse. So far Emme's surgery is going well," Lydia continued with her update. "They've located and retrieved the bullet. Ethan is being debriefed and will be here as soon as he's cleared. Our management team is headed into the office, so it's all hands on deck. We need to get the fans to leave as soon as possible for safety concerns."

Absorbing all her details, I steeled myself for a press conference I wanted no part in. "This isn't what I do," I mumbled softly, the invisible strings keeping me in place finally giving way. I swayed forward, stumbling as I barely caught myself before face-planting on the cold tiles.

Lydia's hand wrapped around my arm, attempting to help me stand up. "She's a fighter," she whispered. "She'll find her way back to you. She has your back. You should go have hers."

Silence overtook us momentarily, finally broken by Lydia's phone chiming multiple times. Looking at the screen, she sighed heavily, "I need to go give our statement."

"I am okay," my voice was firm as I answered her unspoken question. "Where is the press set up?"

She motioned toward the main entrance and I nodded, taking a deep breath and walking with her toward the circus waiting. Emme and I always called it the ring. There was so much noise when Lydia and I walked up and I cleared my throat, ready to be done with this show.

"Ladies and gentlemen," I started strongly. "We know you're here for a statement on the incident tonight and the condition of Emmeline Jones. Currently, all I can relay is that she's still in surgery. The medical personnel have not informed me of anything else, but we are hopeful Ms. Jones will fully recover. What I do know is that during Ms. Jones' final concert of the tour, she was struck by a bullet from a high-powered rifle. Details on the attack are unfortunately murky."

I paused, attempting to steady myself with a deep breath. "While the police are still investigating, right now it is unclear how a gunman entered the stadium or who this attacker is. LJ Productions will work with the police to make sure whoever is responsible is brought to justice under the fullest extent of the law."

I stopped again under the pretense of letting the reporters take their notes and snap their pictures. Mostly I did it because I was wavering. The lights from the cameras were blinding, I felt suffocated in the small circle ... I was ready to check on Emme.

This was a formality, but the gravity of talking about Emmeline right now was nearly impossible to bear. My job—my duty—was to keep her safe. I am supposed to be the one who ensures things like this do not happen. From the moment Emme came into my life, I vowed to protect her. This time I failed. How could these people expect me to speak about how she was doing when this was all my fault?

"Look," I sighed, letting my facade crack just a bit. "Emme would be grateful to know how supportive her fans are, but for tonight, we're asking everyone to please go home. It's been a long day for all of us and we've witnessed a traumatic event. I implore everyone to get some rest. Right now, Emme needs privacy. She needs her family around her. And she needs whoever is responsible for this to be found. That is all for now."

As I turned away, I instantly regretted how I addressed Emme informally in front of the press ... and how I mentioned family. They were two rules I was never meant to break. We never wanted the outside world to know how close we actually were. And we never mentioned family. There was no family; just the two of us.

The noise reached vibrating levels as the voices of the reporters rang out, peppering me with questions. But Lydia and I entered the hospital without acknowledging them further. In the silence that greeted us inside, we walked back toward ICU without a word to each other.

"What can I do for you?" Lydia asked softly after we had arrived back in the safety of the waiting room, free from the prying eyes. She watched as I dropped down into a chair.

"Rewind time," I said dryly, lifting my eyebrows to show I was trying.

She sat on the edge of the chair beside me and leaned into my body. There was a familiarity in the way she placed her head on my shoulder. A not-so-distant memory tugged at my heart—just as quickly as it hit, however, it was gone, interrupted by a phone in my pocket chiming faintly.

"Her phone is blowing up like always," I murmured. It was strange how such a simple thing made me feel so comforted. Emme's phone should be chucked out a window. It screamed at all times, always emitting a new noise from its permanent position in her hand. There were so many times I cursed her for having it. But tonight it made me feel better; closer to her.

"How about I try to find someone who will give me an update?" Lydia responded as she stood from her seat.

I supposed she felt as useless as I did, just sitting and being so close to me. She looked at her phone and sighed before walking off.

"Lydia," I said, catching her attention as she paused to listen. "Thank you. I know you are doing all you can."

She nodded. "I'll be back," she said and took off down the hallway.

I could tell by her posture she heard my voice's sincerity. Our breakup had been hard since neither of us left the company. It took a lot of time with many rocky moments, but finally, we learned how to be in each other's world and have balance. We both slipped back into the gray area tonight—needing someone to lean on.

I let my head fall back as I waited for her to return. For a doctor to come to tell me any news. Or for someone to pop out and tell me this was all a sick joke and we could all go home now.

I wasn't sure how much time passed before Lydia returned, a slight bounce in her step and my backpack slung over her shoulder.

"I talked to a nurse from ICU. His name was Jake," she said as she came up to my side. "He's going to let you shower in one of the resident dressing rooms. I had Abbi go and get a change of clothes for you, too. We will have another press conference in the morning and I need you to look like you aren't freaking out. Tonight was fine because, well, it was needed. But..."

"We need to control the response," I finished for her. "We can't have the fans freaking out, saying Emme is dead."

"I knew you'd know where I was coming from," Lydia replied, relief clear in her voice..

"The show must go on," I repeated Emme's trite line with more snark than I intended. I thought about how often she said that to make the team act even when a situation didn't look good. How often she said it to encourage and inspire those around her when things weren't going well in practice. Had Emmeline said it earlier tonight when the newest dancer was messing up? I couldn't recall, but given her history...

"Exactly," Lydia said with a small smile on her face. She motioned for me to follow her, so I rose from the waiting room chair I'd been camped out in. There was a male nurse waiting at the room Lydia guided me toward; obviously Jake. Once his eyes landed on Lydia, he smiled brightly. It was clear how she snatched this favor for me now.

"This isn't allowed, so please be as quick as possible. If anyone comes in, please say Dr. Drake okayed this," Jake explained.

"Who's Drake?" I asked.

"The lead surgeon on Ms. Jones's case. He'll be in surgery for a bit longer, so no one will question this for a while. You should be fine to get a shower in and get dressed," Jake explained.

"Thank you so much, Jake," Lydia said, smiling as I entered the room behind him.

Hearing her flirt with him as I stepped into the privacy of the washroom made me chuckle. The sound died in my throat when I saw my reflection. It was the first time in hours I had looked at myself.

My shirt was coated with dry blood, my face splattered with it, and my blond hair tinted crimson. My skin was pale, and I wondered if I had aged 10 years during the last few hours. I couldn't remember the last thing I ate or where my stupid water bottle was. I realized now more than before how my reflection showed that my outward appearance matched the inner mess I felt.

Emme went down and I immediately rushed to the stage doing whatever I could to help her. It made sense to see her blood on me. But it didn't make it any easier to handle seeing it everywhere. I stripped my clothes off as quickly as I could, pushing those thoughts far from my mind as I could get them. I mechanically went through the motions of showering, scrubbing every inch of myself and ignoring the rust-colored water circling the drain. My mind kept forcing me to relive the moment Emmeline went down on stage. Guilt bubbled back up in my throat.

It was my job to protect her; it was a part of our pact to each other. Since we started this journey together, we promised to protect each other, to have each others back at all times. Yet, I failed.

How did anyone manage to get a *weapon* into the stadium? That question plagued me more than anything else. Had I not been strict enough with the security team? Was there someone hiding in the stadium before our teams arrived?

There was no way of knowing, but I would find out. Nothing would stop me from tracking down the shooter and figuring who sent them to hurt her. And when I found them, I would do whatever it took to make it right. This would be reconciled.

Chapter Two

Joseph

Feeling refreshed and more human after a long shower, I took up residence in the ICU waiting room with my laptop and a charging cell phone, thanks to Lydia and my personal assistant, Abbi. They also cared for my clothing, bringing me my everyday dark wash jeans, plain tee, and classic black Chuck Taylors. My body was exhausted, but my mind was working non-stop. The first order of business was getting out a press release. I needed to start working on the message the company was to send to national media outlets as soon as we had an update on Emmeline.

As the COO, I had to be prepared for any outcome, so I created a release for good news and a release for bad news. Things like this were delicate, and I knew I had to take my time, getting the right tone in both messages. I scrutinized every word I typed out, attempting to take on her voice.

The first release I tackled was simple; she's okay. She will need privacy and time, but she will recover with an understanding the road will be rough. I would battle her at every turn on this outcome; she's too stubborn to heed the doctor's advice and rest.

The second one—that one was nearly impossible. Typing out the words made it more real than I ever wanted to know. With tears in my eyes, I prayed it was not a release I would ever have to use.

Finished with the task, I sent the documents to Lydia, assuming she left to rest somewhere since I hadn't seen her in a while. Rest would not happen for me until I saw

Emmeline and knew she was okay. Instead, I put my nervous energy where she would want it— extinguishing the million little fires that were catching. Working would be for the best. As it stood, the company was only responsible for one minor head injury due to the panic and the mass exit at the venue. There were calls to be made to all the LJ Productions internal departments to see where the failure in security happened to allow the shooter in. We needed to start internal investigations. It was going to be a long process, but starting the wheels was the best thing I could do until someone, heck, anyone could give me an update.

The next thing I needed was for Ethan to get here ASAP. I knew he was with my staff being debriefed, after having been interviewed by the police department. I needed him here; Emme would not lie in this building, vulnerable and unsecured. He was my best guy and her personal bodyguard nine times out of 10. No one would be able to get to her through him.

By the time a doctor came back to the waiting room, I had coordinated all my managers and all processes were moving. There was only one fire still burning, and I would let it until I knew where Emme's condition stood.

The doctor, who I assumed to be Drake, covered in clean, fresh scrubs, glanced over at me, "Mr. MacDonald?"

I looked the man up and down; he seemed older but had obviously taken time to shower before coming to speak to me, which didn't sit well with me. Didn't he know who she was? How important it was that I, of all people, have an update? I nodded in acknowledgement to his question and he immediately closed the distance between us.

"Are you here for Ms. Jones?"

"Yes, sir," I replied. "Been waiting hours for an update."

The doctor didn't acknowledge my complaint and I filed that away to deal with later.

"Ms. Jones has suffered penetrating abdominal trauma," the doctor started. "She has a laparotomy incision in her abdomen."

"Sir," I interrupted. "Please give me the layman's terms; I don't speak *Grey's Anatomy*."

He chuckled, "Okay, she was shot in her abdomen. Which caused significant damage. We had to go in to remove the bullet and its fragments surgically. I believe she will fully recover, barring any complications, but you should know there were a few difficult moments in the surgery. Her body was already exhausted and didn't handle the strain well. But we were able to keep her stable enough to proceed. She should be waking in the next few hours."

I took a deep breath—it was the first time I didn't feel like I was choking on air— and relief flooded my system. "Can I see her?"

I needed to know all the details not only for my job but for my sanity; I needed a new picture in my head. The last time I saw her, she was being carted away with medical staff all over her. Her body was lifeless. The last time I touched her fingers, they were cold. My body shuttered just recalling it again.

"She will be sedated for a while, but you can sit with her," he replied. "Let me get a nurse to check you in with a visitor pass."

He left me alone in the waiting room again, and I began collecting my things. My cell phone was the last item on the table to be returned to my bag. On a whim, I sent two texts.

"She is out of surgery" was the first message sent to an unsaved number.

The second message, "Heading to her room; she's in recovery," was sent to Lydia. I still needed to remove the heart emoji after her name that Emme put there months ago.

Nurse Jake found me and took me to the ICU nurses' desk. After the stupid paperwork was completed, he led me through doors that had previously been the only barrier between me and Emme.

Entering the room, the reality of everything kicked in. My best friend was unconscious, and even though hospital beds are known to be uncomfortable and small, this one dwarfed Emme's frame, making her seem childlike. The standard ICU equipment surrounded her and a heart monitor steadily beeped. A breathing tube was inserted in her mouth. My legs felt like they no longer had bones but jelly, and I scrambled to the bedside chair.

"You scared me," I whispered to her delicately, my full voice not suited for the room. "No more scaring me. I'm not okay with this."

Leaning over in the chair, every emotion I'd suppressed flooded me. I openly cried next to Emmeline Jones as the day finally ended. She could wake up and stop me, but I knew she wouldn't, so the tears continued to flow.

"I can't lose you," I mumbled, burying my face into my hands.

If I didn't get past these emotions, I couldn't be strong for her when she awoke to the storm that arrived on our stoop without any notice. I was her tether in all storms. Not that she needed it, but because she wanted it.

My body rocked from the sobs I had held in since she tumbled backward on the stage. That was when a small hand I knew fell on my shoulder, Lydia's presence behind me familiar.

"I had my breakdown, too," she whispered, her voice breaking.

"How much did you just witness?"

"Just the end, we have updates whenever you are ready."

Reaching up I covered her hand with my own, and after a moment she pulled hers away and went to the only other seat in the room.

"Give it to me," I instructed.

Lydia started with her comments on the press releases then gave the laundry list of needs and items that had to be handled and her order of priority.

My eyes remained settled on Emmeline as the medication and trauma kept her stiff, still, and way too quiet.

"Are you even hearing me?" Lydia's tone was clearly annoyed with my lack of physical signs of paying attention to her.

"Enough," I ground out.

"When will Ethan be here then?" she challenged.

"Trick question. He's already here, talking with the hospital security about protocols."

I could see enough of her frame from my peripheral vision to know she rolled her eyes at me and leaned back in her chair.

"Okay, had to check," she said.

"How's the press?"

"Running the story non-stop, rehashing what you said. They are doing interviews with attendees and personnel but it's all overwhelmingly positive."

"Anything else?"

"Business is steady. Everyone is on deck and ready to do anything that needs to be done." As she spoke, I could hear her pride in the team she and Emme had made—their willingness to get whatever the job might be done for the good of the company.

"Tell them to stand down for the night," I said, finding myself coming back to reality, breaking from the shock of earlier. "We all need to just make it through the night."

We would all have to make it through the night for any of this to be okay. She had to make it. She *would* make it. I would make it through this night. No more breakdowns, no more pity. I would be her tether; we would withstand this storm.

Chapter Three

Emmeline

I wasn't sure how much time had passed from the moment I fell backward and the pain erupted in my body to the point I started thinking coherently again. Still, I knew I could hear Joe speaking with someone, and that was all I needed to know I was okay. If Joe was there, I would be safe and it would be okay.

"The press is having a field day," the woman stated, her warm honey voice familiar—Lydia.

"Let them," Joe replied back.

His voice was husky; he'd been through it. He always sounded like that when he wasn't sleeping.

It was no surprise the press were going crazy over this. They always did when it came to me, and my reluctance to be interviewed tended to ramp that up most of the time. While there was no way to control all the pieces that were printed about me, Lydia and I planned media appearances to be rare, but beneficial for LJ.

While hearing bits and pieces of what Joe was saying to Lydia about the situation with the press, my mind drifted. Some bits and pieces of old memories were coming back to me. I found myself thinking about a sit-down interview with Terri Goodman I had a couple of months before I kicked off my tour.

When Terri posted about the interview, it made headlines for a week. She wrote for *Hollywood Herald*, a national magazine that discussed everything and everyone in the limelight. Lydia wanted me to talk with her because we knew she had serious journalistic credentials. She wasn't just another gossip columnist, but a serious investigative journalist who focused on the entertainment industry. Everyone who sat down with her saw a sales boost in their business. Her ability to take facts and a few hours with a person and turn them into an insightful story that captivated her audience caused a real change. My hesitation lay in the fact that as helpful as she could be, she could be deadly with her platform too. The damage she could do to a company or career was just as effective.

I was a recluse with the press. I smiled on red carpets, gave sound bites here and there but I didn't do press tours. The fact I was sitting down for an exclusive seemed novel. I was generally not looking forward to it, but I would always put the needs of the company over my personal preferences. The company needed the benefits this interview would give. I just had to keep Terri on my side.

On the day of the interview, Joe arranged for the Mud House Coffee Shoppe to be closed at 2 p.m. While Terri and I settled into the cozy chairs, my security detail swept the building and posted guards at the doors.

While it was an inconvenience for the coffee shop, I had chosen the venue for its environment. If I had to do an interview I was going to be comfortable. And I knew LJ would make sure the shop was fairly compensated for its hassle.

"Thank you for taking time for this, Ms. Jones," Terri said, her tone professional and polite. She was seated across from me, looking professional but with a style all her own.

"My pleasure," I replied, a sugar-sweet smile plastered on my face. There was no way I'd let her or anyone know this was the part of the job I hated more than anything else. I was going to keep the focus on the company and its projects, to ensure the best outcome out of this situation. The article would be published in the next few months and if all went well, it would get people talking and more interested in my next project.

"Maxwell, will you get me a peppermint tea and Ms. Goodman..." I turned to the interviewer, "Would you like anything?."

"Black coffee, please," Terri requested.

As my personal assistant, Maxwell generally traveled with me—helping keep all my ducks in a row—as we managed a career and company. It was a team effort with Raylynn holding down the fort at the office.

My attention came back to Terri as she set up her voice recorder and adjusted the tablet in her hands, "Let's get down to business, shall we?" The sooner we could start, the sooner the hour I'd promised her would be up.

"We shall," I replied, shifting in my seat to try to be as relaxed as possible.

"First I want to be clear about what your expectation is for this piece, Ms. Jones, because, as you know most of my pieces are not only focused on the work of the person I'm speaking with but their personal lives as well. And until today, you have been a big fish who no one could get to sit down and do this with. Why now?"

Terri was clearly at ease, no matter the situation. She received her mug from Maxwell with a smile on her face.

There was no beating around the bush—I was in for a penny and the pound it would seem.

"Well clearly, my personal life is not something I share because of the boundaries I created for myself," I started. "But I wanted to sit down to make an announcement about my career and the LJ Production Company. Knowing how serious you are with your work, I thought it would be best to trust you with this announcement." I wanted to give her the truth without insulting anyone or other publications.

She kept her professional composure, butI could see the surprise flicker across her face.

"I hope that doesn't change your plan for this interview," I said in an attempt to let her have a minute to think about her approach again.

"No, not at all," she replied confidently. "I'll go through what I had prepared and then you can reveal your announcement."

"Sounds perfect to me," I answered, faking my confidence as I leaned back against the chair, steadying myself. Part and parcel of the Emmeline Jones package was the bold confidence my fans looked up to.

Terri sat her drink down, tapping her tablet awake, and picked up her pen.

"LJ Productions is a company you founded with Joseph MacDonald in 2001. When you started, it was just the two of you and now it's a multimillion-dollar company—tell me how you accomplished that without a business degree or any apparent training."

Her voice had no malice, but I could feel the dig; the attempt to stir my emotions. I propped myself up with my elbow, my fingertips grazing my collarbone. An old habit and my only physical tell when I was anxious or frustrated. My face could be unreadable if I wanted it to be, like I did now. Currently, I was CEO Emmeline, and she was the version of me I was best at being. Terri would only see what I wanted her to see. I just had to keep my words matching the persona.

"As you know Terri," I said calmly. "There is no degree needed to be an entrepreneur. However, I had a private education that taught me all the needed business skills," I told her directly. "As those records are not public, I can assure you personally that both myself and Joseph have completed all the hours to earn an MBA in business administration and the proper certifications in accounting, marketing, and finance." I wanted to clap back at her, but I knew I needed to keep the peace, so I kept my tone neutral. "Also, all my extracurriculars in school focused on arts, music, and theater. Would you like the contact of the dance school I attended in NYC?"

"Yes, please," she said without missing a beat, her voice hopeful at the chance to gain more personal information. "How long have you and Mr. MacDonald been associates?"

"Joseph and I have been life-long associates," I answered, glancing over at Maxwell as he wrote down my school's contact information. She wouldn't get much from them—I paid a hefty amount for the school officials to be vague about my time there.

"Several publications have reported the two of you having a romantic relationship as well as a business one," she pressed.

If I could have gotten away with rolling my eyes at the implication, I would have. It felt like some gossip rag was blasting Joe and me as the current couple every other week. Or worse, a couple that was fighting and on the verge of bankrupting the company.

"The fact you two own several homes together fuels that fire. Care to comment on that?" She added to her question as if she could get anything other than my standard answer out of me.

"Mr. MacDonald and I have been lifelong friends and business partners."

"Are you saying there have never been any fleeting romances, as many gossip magazines have reported?"

No matter what I said, people would assume what they wanted. Mostly because of how close Joe and I were. The gossip didn't just end at the magazines, though—the office gossip always hit on what our romantic status was. We didn't do ourselves any favors, especially when Joe would escort me to events as a date. Nor did I ever chase guys, always declining advances from other men and, frankly, women. Joe had girlfriends here and there, but many people dismissed that as cheating or a separation between us.

"Joseph and I were raised together," I countered. "While he is not blood by birth, he is my family." That felt like a safe answer. I tried to keep my posture relaxed while Terri scribbled her notes, but talking about the history Joe and I shared always made me nervous to expose anything that shouldn't be.

Terri leaned forward and my heart sank—I opened the door for her and she was ready to strike. My fingers grazed my collar again and I took a deep breath, trying to not let her see any nerves.

"I've done my due diligence and in my research, you have never discussed anything about your family or childhood,"she stated factually, "But you and Mr. MacDonald were raised together?"

"Yes." It was my first slip-up with the press that I could ever remember. My heart raced and I attempted to backtrack and change the course of this conversation, "Joseph and I were raised in the same neighborhood and ended up at the same art school." While this was a stretch of the truth, it was close enough to go with. "That's where we created the concept of LJ."

"Oh," she started. "You typically never want to discuss history–why?"

"I wouldn't say I never talk about it, just that I prefer to focus on the here and now."

"Tell me about the neighborhood you grew up in," she pressed.

"I'd imagine it was like everyone's neighborhood. Adults worked, kids played." I needed to change the course of this interview immediately. "It seems no matter where we travel for work, I see everyone has a baseline of the same childhood."

"Will you elaborate on any particular memory of your childhood?"

"I had an extraordinary childhood; I had a private education that has given me the means to do what I do today. My memories are cherished keepsakes I never want to forget but my childhood is my past. I have to focus on my future. I want to continue to build a life that is full of memorable moments."

This wasn't the answer Terri wanted, and I knew it. She pulled back and looked at her tablet. "A private education and lessons for voice, theater, and dance. Seems like someone wanted to set you up for the path you are on. Is that why you pursued a career in the entertainment industry at such a young age?"

I picked up my cooling tea from the table to give myself a moment to redefine my answer. I was dancing on a slippery slope, but I had to give her something even if I couldn't talk about my past at all. I had to stick to the script Joe and I memorized from the start of our company.

Terri flicked her pen against her tablet, her impatience with me obvious.

"A business path was always one I was going to take, but I just felt I belonged in the world of art. LJ Productions allowed me to have both. Even if I am not actively acting or performing, I get to work with those who are."

Terri blinked her frustration but followed the natural progression of the great inquisition. "Lillian James Productions is now home to a number of musical artists and is rumored to have more television/movie/streaming shows on the horizon while other production companies' numbers are continuing to drop. What can you attribute that success to?"

"We are not a typical production company," I answer with a small smile, happy to have her back on track. "Specifically when it comes to our musical artists. They can record how they please. Our contracts are like no others in the industry. My contract, for instance, allows me to only do one record every two years. I also tour every two years. This allows me to pursue other avenues. Each of our artists has the freedom to make the best album they can create. Their fans appreciate that. And when we bring in a new artist, we know fan loyalty will help grow the company." I paused to take a moment to sip on my tea.

Sitting my cup back down, I continued, "At other labels, artists have less artistic control. There is more of the mindset of non-stop work to produce more consumable content. That may be changing in the industry now, but as a whole, we are one of the few labels that give their artists the freedom to produce the music they dream of."

"And the other side of the business?"

Terri's was no longer looking relaxed, he jaw was set, and her brow was furrowed, she was going to find a way to circle back to my person life.

However, at this question, I relaxed more. LJ was my heart and home, so talking about business was the easy part. "I know it's the party line for most, but,we take the time to let the actors get into their roles. It's more than just creating for the consumer—which we do—but creating room for the actor to thrive as well. Many actors will leave one of our sets for the first time and realize how different we run a production."

Terri nodded as she scribbled on her tablet, "Giving actors such a free reign, does that ever create issues with directors?"

"Our directors know going into a project we value what actors study and their opinions of the role they are playing. This is why pre-production lasts longer, much longer in our process but because our end result is such a high quality. It's worth it. No matter the script, story, or project, there is time in pre-production to create and work through the vision and goal. Having actors participate in that produces cohesiveness you can see in our final product."

"I see the correlation to the records you are breaking," she conceded. "Why did you and Mr. MacDonald decide to go in such a different direction from other production companies?" There was a sudden smirk on her face that made me wonder what she was expecting.

The direct answer was because of our education, and her smirk told me that she knew that. We knew you had to have everyone buy-in for a successful business. But Terri was looking to dig into the past again with this question. I had to get her back into the present and stay away from whatever she was searching for.

"It's about the buy-in," I simply said.

"The buy-in?" she repeated incredulously leaning back in her seat again.

"I feel like I could compare it to you writing an article. Not that I presume to know your process, but I believe you want your readers to lean into your topics. So you create the headline to grab their attention. Then lead them to buy into the topic, so they will read the whole story."

Terri's face furrowed while I continued. "When we approach a project as producers, I clearly have to buy in. Then the director has to love it and have a vision for it. Each actor has to buy into the project as well; that's why we do the extended pre-production. We get all the buy-in. Then the vision is set and we can move forward."

Terri considered my comparison, and I could see on her face we were *finally* going to move forward with the conversation. Still, I knew she was far from giving up.

"Do you want to strictly stay in the production/talent lane?"

"I would like to say yes. I've thought about it. But really, who doesn't think about different ways of furthering a career? However, I currently have no plans for it. Being a producer gives me the time I need for all my responsibilities. I'm not sure I'm willing to give that up for a short-term project," I answered. It was easy because I had thought about doing other things, namely directing. I just never found the right reason to step away to take the time for a directing spot.

"LJ Productions is not the only company you have founded, correct?"

"It is not," I nodded. She was going to ask about Angel Wings, the only venture I ever did without Joseph's support.

"Tell me about Angel Wings."

"It is a non-profit I founded about six years ago for children of addicts."

"Your organization helps so many but you don't oversee the day-to-day operation."

"No, I don't." I paused. She didn't ask a question and I didn't want to offer anything I shouldn't. This woman already unwittingly had me open a door for her. It was important to speak very carefully.

"Why?" she asked, her eyebrows lifting up her forehead.

"It's simply a matter of time," I replied swiftly.

"When you founded the non-profit, you were quoted as saying how important it was to support the children of those who had turned to drugs. If it's that important, then why did you turn over the day-to-day operations?" Terri asked sharply, leaning back in towards me.

"Because it is that important," I replied sincerely. "As CEO of LJ, a million little fires, papers, scripts, proposals make it to my desk. Angel Wings needs to be given full attention by a capable CEO in order for it to be an effective organization. I was very thorough in the hiring process. The foundation is in very capable hands."

"How often do you check in?"

"I attend every stakeholder board meeting, and I have daily reports to have an understanding of how the foundation is doing."

"Of all the causes you could have created an organization for, why the children of drug users?"

My heart skipped a beat, "Children are so innocent. When they have parents who choose highly addictive substances, they get lost in an overrun system. I wanted them to have more support."

"Is there a personal connection to this cause for you?" Terri was fishing again, her eyebrow had arched with the question.

"My first movie, we had a young girl on set daily," I started. "As I got to know her, she shared her story with me.

I just kept thinking, 'Wow, this girl has overcome so much without help—what could she have done with support?'"

Terri concentrated on her notes and tablet as I spoke, a clear tactic for more, so I continued.

"I kept going back to her and her story and I just never forgot it. I decided to do something about the next child who faced her situation."

There was a part of my brain that knew she'd take this answer and be fine, but another part worried if she were to dig deeper.

"As a young person, new in the circus of fame, you were impacted?" Terri confirmed.

"I was. Mallory's story never left me and when I could, I created Angel Wings."

Terri again leaned back, satisfaction written all over her face, so I went on. She felt she had won, so I let her take the win. There were multiple reasons for the creation of Angel Wings, and this girl was the reason I finally founded it.

"Mallory could have easily been me. We were close in age, but her upbringing had been very different." I let my gaze drift to the door, thinking about her story. How heavy my heart felt the first time I met Mallory.

"Her father was in a terrible accident and became addicted to painkillers. Her mother didn't cope well and started to partake as well. Not as often as the father, but enough that Mallory was placed in a group home." The familiar ache crept back into my chest as I went over it all. How closely our paths were connected, my eyes filling with tears, the pain, and guilt for Mallory rising again.

"Well, it's her story and I've already said enough, but I just couldn't ever forget it." I let the tears fall and Maxwell quickly appeared at my side with a Kleenex. I sniffed and dried my tears.

"The foundation was a long time coming and it's because of her. I've kept in touch with Mallory through the years, and she has her own company now, doing great things."

Terri smiled, "I had no idea. That is why I love storytelling. You never know how a story will impact you."

I let my hand rest in my lap—I had finally won Terri over. I gave her a personal detail that was completely true, even if it wasn't the full story, and it satisfied her curiosity.

Terri tapped her tablet with her pen again, "Tell me who is Emmeline. Who are you?"

Sharply inhaling through my nose, the room felt like it was starting to spin. My thoughts faltered. What could she mean? Who am I? What does she know? My limbs twitched, I needed to run. But, the heaviness in my body left me paralyzed in place.

"Meaning?" I answered her question with one of my own, keeping my voice even, trying to find the context of what she was implying.

"What do you do in your personal time? What are your hobbies? What activities do you do when you aren't working? Who is Emmeline when she's not a rockstar, CEO, philanthropist?"

Again spinning, the panic that seeped in so quickly, suddenly started to vanish. My body would take an hour to fully relax, but at least I knew that she didn't know anymore than the average joe. This is why I hated the press, I never knew their true intentions.

"Ummm," I stuttered, "There are functions I'm invited to attend. There are benefits, red carpets, galas, and other things. I also tend to do much of my writing during personal time." I paused, "Although that is under that work label."

Terri kept her expression fairly neutral, waiting for more. I had to center myself. Stressing myself was exhausting. My fingertips pressed into the hard bone in my collar again.

"Outside of all the work," I said, smiling at her again, "is cooking."

"Cooking," Terri repeated.

Taking a deep breath, and holding it for a moment to calm all the anxieties, I continued. " I host a family dinner at my home once a month."

"What do you consider a family dinner?" Terri poked, keeping the probing look.

"I love to cook and try new recipes, and experiment with different styles and types of food. So once a month, I invite whoever I'm working with or friends in the area to come and dine with me. We'll sit down together, catch up and share stories over a home-cooked meal. It's a time to relax and just enjoy the company of others versus working all the time."

"I bet you've had quite a few spectacular dinners with many amazing people."

"My table is open to those who I invite and a stray comes in every now and then," I joke lightly. "But yes, it makes for some amazing moments." I couldn't help but laugh as a multitude of memories jumped to the front of my mind, though I refrained from sharing. Throwing my friends under the bus with a ridiculous story wasn't what I wanted to do ever.

"And other than cooking?" Terri pushed.

"Nothing really," I shrugged. "I'm just a girl who works too hard and loves to cook and write. I travel for both pleasure and work."

"What motivates your writing?" she asked, scribbling away and looking for something specific.

"Everything, anything, and nothing at all," I said quickly. "Writing is a place where I can be cathartic with emotions. Or just make things up and be creative. It's the best of both worlds."

Terri clearly wanted me to circle back to my childhood in any way she could find—asking about the reasons behind my choices and whatnot. But I continued to refuse to go back to that closed conversation. When I did not elaborate anymore, she looked through her notes, and then back to me.

"That's all I had," she stated without looking at me. She took a moment more to flip through her before looking back up at me, a bit of smugness written all over her face, "All that's left is your announcement."

I hadn't given her anything I didn't want to, so I wasn't so sure why she looked as if she won some game.

"Oh, that, " I replied with a small coy smile. I shifted in my seat, my tea long gone, and looked at Maxwell for a second. His warm smile gave me a spike in confidence I didn't know I needed.

"After balancing two movies, three TV show launches, and using every spare second I had, my next album is now ready to launch."

"Well, that's exciting," Terri breathed out, not sounding excited at all. Slumbing back into her seat. I wasn't sure what she had been expecting, but my next album just wasn't it, clearly.

"Yes, I'm very pleased about the release of my seventh studio album, *gAme on*, which will be released the same night as the first show of the *gAme on' Tour*," I added.

"Excuse me, did you just say a new tour?" she deadpanned, there was the spark of excitement I wanted.

"Yes, ma'am," I said with glee. "My schedule had been so consumed after my last tour, we weren't sure if the company could afford to have me managing my role, so far away from my desk. While we all managed, it was difficult. Joseph and I went through many applicants and have found an excellent addition to the company, rather than balance my roles from the road, I'll be able to step away for a bit and know the company is in good hands. I've been able to delegate all my roles for the next two years."

"A two-year tour?"

"Unfortunately, no. Just 18 months. The first six months will be used for intense rehearsal. I've had my musical team working for months on all the prep work and pre-production for the tour in secret."

It took so much planning and preparation to create a world tour in confidentiality, but once Terri's article hit the newsstands, all the non-disclosure agreements would be nullified and my stress levels would lessen significantly.

"First stop?" she asked, being sure to get the pertinent details.

"First and last stop will be the Ronald Adams Exhibition Stadium."

"First and last?" Terri continued to scribble quickly.

"Yes, a little treat for my hometown crowd." My smile reached my eyes in a way that made me blink a little.

"That is exciting."

"We have a list of all the currently scheduled dates and venues, with the hope to add more," I added, Maxwell appearing at Terri's side once I spoke and handed her a manilla folder with a copy of the schedule and the press release Lydia created, as well as all the artwork for the tour and new music. "If you need any additional info please contact my office directly."

"What can you tell me about the tour?" she probed, looking for more than it's happening.

"The whole album tells one story of a bounty and her hunter. So the tour will have a real cat-and-mouse feel about it. From the dancing to the lights, this tour will have an exciting story to tell."

I watched Terri process that information, and then check her watch.

"Thank you so much for your time," Terri said, extending her hand.

I returned her handshake, "Of course, thank you for your time as well."

"I do have further research and interviews before I will publish the article," Terri explained to me, gathering her supplies.

"Of course," I say, returning my teacup to the counter.

"Most likely this will be broken down into two separate pieces. I'll have the announcement out by the next publication."

"I appreciate that. If you need anything else, please don't hesitate to contact my office," I repeated.

My personal guard Ethan then guided the reporter out of the shop and while I waited for his return, Maxwell handed my phone to me.

"You have 18 text messages, one voicemail, and a very needy Joe wanting to know how this went. I talked to him twice. And then of course, there are your social alerts and media accounts."

"Thank you, Max," I smiled. My phone was constantly blowing up, which Joe always criticized me about. But this was just a fact of life. I had to keep things up-to-date. Though knowing how nervous Joe was always made me smile.

I swiped right on Joe's name in my contacts, the line ringing immediately.

"Joe's phone," he answered robotically.

"Hey."

"Oh, hey," he paused. "How'd it go?"

"Oh, it was good. She had some very intriguing questions."

"Are we a couple again?" he questioned.

"We'll have to wait and see, but potentially. She asked a lot about our relationship."

"Great. Jennifer and I have been talking again. Do you know how hard it is to convince someone that I'm not dating my business partner when it's all over every entertainment news outlet?"

I laughed, "I'll be sure to tell her I don't want to sleep with you."

"Great, thanks," Joe replied dryly. "That'll help, I'm sure."

I returned to the office after that, knowing it would be a long wait until I could see what Terri and her paper would print. I could only hope I had given her enough personal facts to make an excellent feature. I knew the details on LJ's film projects would generate the buzz I wanted. And people would definitely talk about our new vice presidents and a world tour would get my fans buzzing. The more I thought back over the interview, however, the more something felt off.

A harsh beeping broke through my thoughts and something shifted. I wasn't at my desk anymore, but still in the coffee shop, watching Maxwell leading Terri out of the coffee shop. She had wanted something I didn't give her.

"She was fishing," I said simply as Maxwell made his way back to me. I sighed and pressed a hand to my forehead. My brain felt fuzzy, and my voice sounded off as I spoke the words. It sounded like I had swallowed gravel and caused a sharp vibrating pain in my throat. Really, my throat felt like fire. My consciousness shifted again and I was positive now something was off. Things were too silent—I realized I was no longer in the coffee shop. Was I on stage?

No—but I had been. What was the beeping? Nothing was normal. Where was Joe? Wasn't I just with Maxwell?

"Is she awake?" Lydia asked, her voice sounding hopeful yet tinged with panic.

"No, no I'm not—not really," I thought to myself. I was awake enough to hate the sharp pain in my throat. But it was all I felt. I had to think. What was going on?

"Emme, do what?" Joe questioned, his voice eager. "It has to be the morphine. She was breathing so well they removed the tube early this morning and gave her a pain management system."

"She's going to have to feel the pain," Lydia sighed heavily.

"Not today. She doesn't have to today," Joe replied sternly.

Oh, this is bad, I thought. *But I'm safe.* I couldn't focus anymore, already drifting back into my dreamscape, hearing only half of what happened in the world around me, and heading deep into the recesses of my brain. I didn't feel any other pain, but a part of me worried Lydia was right—I would be feeling all kinds of pain soon.

Chapter Four

Emmeline

I focused on the beeps, which drew me back to reality and away from my dreams.

Beep. Beep. Beep.

It kept a steady rhythm and gave me a focus point. I realized then I must have been in and out of conscience for the last few hours.

"What's beeping?" I asked, my voice hoarse and dry as I whispered the question.

"Your heart monitor," Joe dryly replied, rising from his chair to lean over me.

"'Kay." I felt in a haze and attempted to pull myself up.

"Don't think about moving," Joe caught me, touching my shoulders lightly but firmly enough to keep me from jostling too much. "You don't want to tear open your incision."

"Joe, what's happened?" All the time I swirled around in my brain, I could never pinpoint what had actually happened to me. I knew the pain felt horrible. I remember seeing the blood vividly from my apparent wound, but my brain couldn't process any valid answers.

"You're at St. Catherine's; you were shot," Joe explained. "Do you remember what happened at all?"

Clamping my eyes shut, I felt his eyes watching me. I had been floating around in my head undirected but now that I was thinking, I remembered how I stumbled backward after a mind-numbing pain ripped through my stomach. I recalled each second it took security and Joe to respond, the sound of my blood pumping in my ears. Clearly, I recalled Joe's frantic expression as he placed his hands on my abdomen.

Opening my eyes, I sighed heavily, "I just remember performing but not finishing the show."

Reading the relief on his face he murmured, "That's probably best for now." My best friend briefly closed his eyes and drew a deep breath through his nose.

My condition was bad enough that he didn't call me on my lie, or he didn't hear it. But I wanted to protect him as much as I could; he was probably tearing himself apart because this happened. I was so sleepy, and keeping my eyes open, no matter how brief, had exhausted me.

Falling back into a dreamscape, I followed the sound of a voice down a hallway. Allowing my brain to lose track again of what was actually happening, I found myself in more happy places. Thinking about the pain wasn't something I wanted to do right now.

It could have been a moment later or days, I wasn't sure, but I could suddenly hear Lydia talking shop again.

"I've been fielding a ton of calls from everyone," she started. "What?" I worked with them both long enough to know he was shooting her some sort of face that made her stop short.

"She doesn't need visitors; she needs rest," Joe snapped. For him it was simple, my health above all else. The truth was, I didn't even know what sort of shape I was currently in, so I had to trust him to make the right call.

"I know," she paused. "But..."

"But nothing," Joe hissed at her.

He was rougher with her than he would typically allow himself to be. I hoped she could take care of him because it was clear I would not be able to for now.

"Her family wants to know how she is doing," Lydia whispered back. I didn't miss her small sniff at the end. Joe had been too harsh again.

"What have you been telling them ?" His tone was accusatory.

"Look, I don't need that," Lydia's voice dropped, her own accusatory tone coming forth. Things had apparently been tense between them since the shooting.

"What?" he huffed at her.

"You are being so short with me. I get you are scared, but I'm in this with you, not against you."

"I'm not. I don't...I just can't deal with them right now."

"You are under a lot of stress. I get that," she paused and took a breath. "But stop snapping at me."

"She doesn't need visitors," Joe reiterated, this time more gently. "Tell them she's recovering and when she can, they can visit in small doses."

"I *have* been telling them she's resting," Lydia said, and I could hear the smile in her voice as a response to his tone change.

"Anything else?"

"Just that they can show their support on social media. Keep the hashtag trending."

"Do you ever stop working?" Joseph asked, a lightness in his voice now.

"Only when I'm asleep."

"When this is over, remind me we must adjust your pay scale."

I could only assume Joseph realized how lucky we were to have her. Lydia had been pivotal in transforming our company from a start-up to a contender in the industry. She had the right eye and spunk to make LJ what it had become.

"Definitely will remind you of that," Lydia responded.

The pair went quiet and my mind started thinking of my friends. They had to be worried sick. Nothing like this had ever happened, and they were all a bunch of worry warts. We were more than work colleagues, in fact, they

40

were more my family than any blood relative I ever had. I kept them close with family dinners and hanging out outside of work events. I wanted to have them around to keep laughter in my home.

A memory came to the surface and took over my mind's eye. I found myself in my kitchen with Lydia and Raylynn while the house was bustling with the sounds of the family I'd made for myself on a dinner night.

"You stay out," I shouted at Joseph in the memory when he started through the pocket doors that separated the kitchen from the dining room. He froze in his tracks, threw his hands up as surrender, and slowly backed out of the door frame.

The girls laughed as he slipped away. Putting on the finishing touches of the meal, the ladies began to serve it in the dining room.

"Dinner time!" Raylynn shouted outside to the porch while Lydia informed those in the living room.

After a few minutes, the table in the dining room was full of the ones Joe was now keeping at arms length. They should be close to me, they'd want to be.

"Okay, we have a new face," I announced as I settled into my spot, "so we need introductions."

"You don't have to do anything, on my account," the scruffy-faced man sitting directly to the right of me said.

"Nope, house rules," Joseph replied matter-of-factly from his seat at the other end of the table.

"I'll start," a redheaded man somewhere in the middle of the table jumped up. "I'm Shawn. I've known Emmeline since she graced the town with her presence. We have been in a few productions together, most recently Stale Popcorn."

"I'm next, I suppose," a woman to Shawn's right said. "I'm Katy, this goof's best friend," she paused to point at Shawn.. "Emme and I have been friends for as long as him. We only worked on one movie together. But it's been good to have her around to learn things with."

The rest of the guests went round-robin until it reached the newcomer.

"I'm Austin, the newbie," the man said. He was tall and reminded me of a cowboy. He had that sort of gruffness about him, though he didn't have a background of being a real cowboy. "I'm here because I will be co-producing Ms. Jones' next album."

There was a tiny gasp from Katy, "I didn't think you were capable of delegating."

Joe gave Austin a very long look before he turned his attention to me, "I didn't know you were hiring a co-producer on this upcoming album."

"It was a last-minute choice," I answered. "We have Chris and Eloise's new movie, and we will be filming while I am recording."

I gave him a nonchalant shrug as he read my face and when he saw what he needed, he turned back. "Welcome to the crazy, Austin."

"Thanks, man." Austin replied, having watched the interaction between Joe and I carefully.

"Tell us about you," Katy piped up.

"I've been producing independent artists for four years now," Austin responded as dinner commenced. "Music has been my passion for more years than I can count."

He had easily charmed the group as he talked about his production approach, and they welcomed him with open arms. Really, all they needed to accept him was to say he was good to be there.

Dinner was full of loud conversations and bickering that only happens when you put friends together. During the round of second helpings, Raylynn and Lydia got up to serve the pies ordered from a local bakery. I loved these pies, and it always made me happy when I could support the small businesses, since I was that once.

As dinner came to a close, Joseph pulled me to the side, out of sight of the prying eyes and ears of my friends who headed to the backyard for the rest of the night.

"You have never hired a co-producer," he stated in an accusatory low voice.

"Which makes you angrier, that you didn't know or you didn't vet him?" I asked bluntly, feeling his irritation vibrating off him.

"Both." He ran his hand over his face, and then leaned in and whispered, "Why would you trust a stranger with your lyrics?"

"I don't and I'm not." I sighed, "Kramer called me at the office this morning."

Joseph's face ashened, and his whole body went ridged. Kramer was not someone we openly spoke about—no matter how much he ran our lives. He was the unseen string puller, doing things for us no one else could have ever done.

"He sent Austin here. He wants me to have more *oversight*," I whispered, glancing around to make sure we were still having a private conversation.

I watched as his face shifted into anger, his shoulders tensing. "We need to talk then when everyone leaves."

"I know. There wasn't time before this dinner, but that's why Austin is here." I ran my hand down his arm, "We haven't had time for a conversation, let alone one that is needed. "

"So Kramer sent him in for oversight, and you are introducing him as a music producer so his proximity is never questioned."

"Exactly," I confirmed. "He'll be around me, more than anyone will like, but I'll be safe. He's also *not* touching my music."

"I don't like this," he started, pulling back from our bubble.

"We don't..." I started to reply but was interrupted as a loud crash and glass shattering was heard echoing through my home.

"I'm okay," a deep voice bellowed.

"What did you do?" Katy asked as I scurried to my living room.

Glass shards coated the floor and a mirror frame previously hanging on my wall was busted all over the floor. Chris, a hulking man, lay in the center of the broken glass.

"How'd you manage this?" Eloise, his wife, asked him as she entered the room.

"I'd rather not say," he chuckled. He stood and carefully removed himself from the glass scattered on the floor.

"Just look at this mess," I mumbled out loud, somewhere between my living room and the hospital room with Lydia and Joe, who had moved back to a bedside chair.

"What mess?" Lydia asked me while I blinked my eyes opened slowly.

When I was fully back in the present, I let my work brain take over, "Nothing, just run it down for me. What's going on?" My voice was steady now, sounding like the CEO I was.

Joseph responded to me as if it was compulsory. "Press conference was held, and your updated condition was shared with fans, stated at the time that you are expected to make a full recovery. The police were urged to find the shooter fast. Camp asked for privacy to allow you time to heal and recover."

His voice was hard, sounding just like my COO Joseph MacDonald.

"Who spoke?"I asked, closing my eyes again to listen to his responses.

"Me, of course."

"Did you stutter?"I asked jokingly.

"No, but I did wear my blood-stained shirt," he responded nonchalantly.

"Well, that makes an impression," I groaned. "Good job."

"Lydia has been monitoring all social media sites and media outlets. It's all good, positive responses," Joseph continued.

"Okay, that's all I need right now." My eyes stayed closed, and my voice started to fade again.

"Rest, Emme," Joe said softly. "I've got your back."

My best friend was back with me, so I did.

Chapter Five

Joseph

I watched Emme, turning my phone in my hands as I had been doing for the last few hours. After she fell back asleep, I'd decided to send a text message to someone I didn't want to be involved in the current situation, but also knowing that I had to let him know she was still alive. Even if that wasn't what he wanted to hear.

I expected the text to prompt a call quickly, but deep down, I knew he would want to be sure I had the full details before he could rake me over the coals. My guilty conscience would be nothing compared to the blame this man would throw my way. Plus, I knew my public statement about her family would be taken as an invitation. I shouldn't have given it, but at the time, I felt obligated to provide the information and open the door to them.

The theme song from "The Walking Dead" suddenly began to play on my phone, and I answered the call without hesitation, "Joe's phone."

"What happened?" a stern, angry male voice demanded from the other end of the line.

"Better question, what did you do?" I demanded, anger flooding my voice without realizing it.

"You can't be blaming this on me," the voice stated in shock.

"I might be," I retorted, holding my position with a firm tone.

Silence crept into the room as the man on the phone seemed to take in the accusation I levied against him.

"Joe?" Emmeline's voice broke into the thick air in the room.

"I've got to go," I snapped, ending the call and taking four steps to be back at Emmeline's side.

"Right now, without any games, who was on the phone?" she demanded of me, her voice still weak.

"I ... I just," I paused and let out a heavy sigh. "No."

"Joseph Matthew, tell me now." Her voice was tired and small but firm.

"Who do you think it was?"

"Was it him?" she asked, her voice wavering.

"Knock, knock," Lydia interrupted as she entered the room. "Is Sleeping Beauty awake right now?"

"Yeah. Barely, but yeah," Emmeline replied, her eyes not leaving mine. I remained mute, hoping I could buy a few minutes alone with my thoughts.

"Has Joe updated you on the business stuff?" Lydia asked, causing Emmeline to break her eye contact with me. But I knew her, and she would file that phone call away to deal with later. She wanted to know who I accused on the phone. No matter what state she was in, she missed nothing.

"He's given me absolutely nothing. Why don't you fill me in?"

"I'll be back. I'm going to get some coffee." It was a poor excuse to get out of the room for a moment, but now that Ethan was standing guard and Lydia was at Emmeline's bedside, I felt I could take a second away.

Closing the door, I heard Lydia rundown all the details of how the press was handling the story, what the police were saying publicly, and how the fans were responding. Even though she was tired, Emmeline would take in each and every detail. And if I had to bet, she would even give a few tips here and there. But in her weird brain, I would be the focus — how I walked away, how I hung up the phone, how I jumped from calm to livid with a few words from the person on the other side of the line.

I made my way down the hall, staying within a reasonable distance. In an attempt to steady myself, I took a heavy breath and then redialed the number I'd answered a few moments before.

The phone rang three times before the male voice answered.

"You better have a good reason for hanging up on me," the man gruffed. He was in a foul mood, but so was I.

"She woke up," I snapped. "I couldn't have her know who I was talking to, now could I?"

"No, you couldn't," the other man stated solemnly.

"I know our arrangement," I snarled, then paused. "Sometimes I think better than you do."

"I also know the arrangement, Joseph," the other voice said. "Things are just a bit tense right now."

"Yes, I know. I am the one who's staying vigilant at her bedside," I replied snarkily.

I wasn't sure if he barked or huffed, but a weird mix of the two noises reverberated through the phone.

I knew this was silly and we were not going to get anywhere. I needed to relay the information about Emme to him. Taking another deep breath, I let the personal stuff go, I was going to be straightforward and hope he would man up and do the same. "Look, she's okay. Well, no, she's not okay, but she will be. Her surgery was successful. She'll recover. She'll be okay. The problem will be keeping her resting to heal."

The other man laughed, "Yes, that sounds about right. She never did like to be still."

"He trained her to be very ambitious and active," I agreed, feeling emotionally spent. So much so it hurt to smile as I spoke the statement. It was a testament to Emmeline how everyone praised her work ethic, and she did it all so pristinely because of her father—he had trained her to be three steps ahead of everyone constantly.

"That he did," the other voice agreed, obviously remembering the training Emme had endured and thrived in.

Sighing, I continued, "Look, you trust me and I trust you, so I need to know ... Was this something you're responsible for?"

"I don't know. I have to tread delicately to find out. I'll call when I know," he replied.

"No, don't call," I commanded. "You need to text. That leaves more of a trail, but she'll know if you call and I answer. She knew I was on the phone with someone earlier."

"Who does she think it was?"

"Does it matter?" I asked dryly. "She knows it was with one of you, and that will be a problem."

"Should I come?" The man sounded needy but hopeful. He wanted me to say yes.

"I don't think that would be wise," I whispered.

"Man, she's my sister; I have seen the footage. I *need* to come. I *need* to see for myself," he said, his biting tone returning.

"No, no, you can't. Jackson, just trust me. Do everything you can to keep her safe from your end, and I'll do the same," I interrupted him firmly.

He let out a harsh breath, "I don't like this."

"You don't have to like it. This is our arrangement. This is what was dictated. You can't see Emmeline," I reiterated.

I immediately ended the call before he could raise his voice; if I had to guess, hearing him attack me again would send me over the edge, and this was not the time or the place.

"Do I want to know what that was about?"

Spinning around, I spotted Lydia standing behind me, watching with hesitation. Shaking my head, I gave her no answer in return.

Lydia didn't linger on the topic, thankfully. "I filled Emme in, and she's resting again." I had to give her credit; she either pretended she hadn't heard me in an intense conversation about Emmeline or wasn't going to berate me more on the issue. "I'm going home, changing, and clocking out for a while," she continued. "Please call me if you need anything, though. I do mean anything. I care about her too."

"Thank you, Lydia," I answered, completely sincere in my reply.

"Goodnight, Boss," the petite woman said, leaving me where she found me, alone with my bad mood and sour thoughts.

The first 36 hours after Emmeline's surgery had not been easy to get through. Even if we were ordinary people, it wouldn't have been easy. But we were not and the added strain of the press releases, damage control, and fans flocking to stand vigil outside the hospital made me feel crazy.

On top of all that, Emme was floating in and out of consciousness. To see her awake enough to catch a phrase or two, say something to me or Lydia, and then be out again before any of us could form a response was exacerbating my foul mood.

As I watched Lydia walk away from me, I felt everything start to crash in. The lies of the past, the hidden truths, and the hurdles we'd moved away from all were pushing their way to the front and center of our lives again. I slowly walked back to Emme's room, my legs heavy and moving my body at a snail's pace; I was so tired.

Sneaking back into her hospital room, I did my best not to wake her and attempted to catch some sleep in the chair beside her. I needed to stay by her side. Because I had this distinct feeling that what had been buried worked its way back to the surface. And I wouldn't leave her side again if I could help it.

Emmeline

I felt like I was awake for longer stretches, though the morphine kept my mind foggy. Dr. Drake wanted to ease me off the pain meds, but Joseph insisted I needed a few more days. He knew I'd push myself way too hard and fast. But healing was a luxury I never allowed myself and I couldn't see how I should now. Which was how Joseph convinced the medical professional he knew better. A slight; I wanted to remember to get him back eventually.

While I knew the time was necessary, I hated it—with everything in me—but I didn't have it in me to fight Joe or the hospital staff.

Three days after I was shot, I was still prone in bed, a combination of the pain, morphine, and my wound keeping me in the hospital. This along with my actions of following the medical staff's instructions said more to Joseph than any words I spoke could—I was still not okay.

I heard the doctors continue to reassure him of my condition—I was healing just fine and would recover. But as he allowed his worry to morph, changing him and making him go overboard out of panic. He was barely leaving the hospital room, making crazy arrangements for security and protection, and I wasn't sure he was eating.

His body fidgeted in ways I hadn't seen in years. I wondered if the whole situation had him slipping back to his old habits to keep calm. His back was to me, as he stood at the window, the blinds open enough that daylight flooded through. I knew the guilt he was feeling and had to get him to back down before he completely broke.

"You are making me crazy," I finally said softly.

"What?" Joseph jumped slightly, as if I startled him, as he turned to face me. I believed he thought I was sleeping again. But maybe he was lost in his own mind, as I had been in my mind so much since I was attacked.

"Look, if you pace that window to the door again, I'm going to make Ethan take you home."

"How do you know Ethan is here?" he asked, facing me with eyebrows raised.

"I've been shot, not rendered senseless. Ethan is always close. Also, I've not always been asleep, I can be quiet and still from time to time."

His hand raked his face, disbelief written across his face. His feet dragged slowly as he came to me, and sat on the edge of my bed. The look in his eyes screamed he was full of concern and self-doubt. While never my cup of tea, Joe was a beautiful man—but I could see how this had impacted him. His face was hollowed, the sleepless nights bringing heavy bags under his eyes. He was in a deep dive into darkness. "The monsters are here now."

"Yes, you silly boy," I giggled and instantly regretted it, wincing in pain. Joe didn't even react, he was missing my red flags that would have normally made him jump. "I've allowed you to do your thing as I've followed the doctor's orders and rested. It's given me a chance to think about things."

Joe looked away from me, his mind clearly preoccupied, his head dropping, a soft sigh escaping him, "I thought I was going to lose you."

For a moment, I could hear all the things we left unsaid. The unspoken bond between us, what made us more than best friends, but less than romantic partners. The bonds we had that tied us to one another for life. I tried to read his face, but he refused to look at me. Had I died, it would have killed him too.

"You did for a minute," I sighed. I didn't mean to say that, but was glad I did when his head jerked to swivel back to make eye contact again, allowing me to see his exhaustion, his fear, and his guilt.

"Doc said it was sketchy," he admitted through gritted teeth.

"I think I coded on the table," I said dryly. "Everything has been so fuzzy I'm not sure what is memory or dream at this point."

"I can imagine this whole thing has been hard on your mind as well as your body," he offered, his body swaying from his exhaustion.

"I just want to sleep and rest," I admitted while adjusting my head placement on the pillow. "And not have to worry about you."

"Don't you dare worry about me," he sighed, pinching the bridge of his nose with his fingers. "As long as you are fine, I will be fine."

"Then please calm down," I reiterated. "You've been making Lydia a nervous wreck and everyone else jittery."

"I'm sorry." Joe tried to stand up, to escape my critical eye.

"You should be," I snorted at him.

Shifting in the bed, I reached for his arm and he allowed me to pull him to a lay next to me, then I hit the morphine button. "Please just lay here and rest."

He didn't answer me, but I could feel his body relax, letting him know that I had won this round. "Also, ease up on the no-visitor rule. It would be nice to see some friendly faces." I didn't wait for an answer as I heard a soft snore escape him, as the morphine took me into another sleep state.

Chapter Six

Emmeline

Alyson Summers stood in front of the backdrop of the gossip channel, MIN News, in a formal business blue dress, and looked into the camera ahead of her.

"Three short days after the shooting at Memorial Stadium, fans and authorities are perplexed by how a gunman entered the facility armed without anyone knowing it. The country is still waiting for more updates on Emmeline Jones's condition from her team."

"Ugh, can she at least sound cheery?" I whined, still stuck in the hospital and forced to watch TV with no work or visitors to keep me busy.

The screen showed standard press photos of me from a red carpet event, one I couldn't quite place. "Lydia needs to get a different photo out to the media. I hate that dress."

"Jones was in the middle of the final concert of her gAme on' Tour when the unknown shooter fired a single round which hit the star in her abdomen and caused extensive damage," the reporter continued. "Jones is known for her roles in *Meeting in the Sun* and *Assistant of the Rose*, as well as various works with her foundation, Angel Wings, which helps impoverished families. She is also the CEO of The LJ Production Company, which has released many blockbuster titles, including *Vampire Love*."

"Why can't they ever name one independent film I've been the lead in?" I asked, huffing. "They could name *Coffee with Mikie*. It wouldn't hurt anything, and that was a profitable film."

"The last statement from Joseph MacDonald, COO of LJ Production Company, advised the media and fans that Jones is currently resting and healing. The company is asking for the public's understanding as she takes time to focus on her recovery."

The blonde reporter changed cameras and continued, "Jones was set to star in and co-produce the upcoming production of the latest spin on *A MidSummer's Night Dream.* There has been no official word on what will happen with the production."

"We will hire another actress to do the work, and I'll still get production credit. That's what will happen, Alyson," I snarkily said. This program was my least favorite, but my remote was out of reach, and I was forced to listen to her discuss my life in an open forum.

"We sincerely hope for the best for Ms. Jones," Alyson ended. No one was in the room to see me stick my tongue out at the TV screen. "When we return, we take a look at Oprah's new favorite things!"Alyson declared, a touch of pep in her voice.

"Seriously, why am I even watching this?" I heaved and punched the pillow supporting my lower back.

"Because you are literally stuck in bed and have no life right now," Chris said as he walked into my hospital room. I hadn't seen him since the family dinner where he replaced the mirror he shattered. He grinned like a puppy that returned a stick. I smiled at the memory.

"Being shot is kind of having a life, unlike crashing into priceless mirrors," I quipped back. "But it's sort of exciting."

Chris came up to my bedside, leaned down, and gave me an incredibly awkward, gentle one-arm hug.

"Well, getting shot is exciting; lying around afterward is another story." He held a vase full of brightly colored flowers that he sat on the window sill."Wifey said you need colors, nothing plain."

"Well, wifey was right; those are beautiful." I smiled. It felt good to smile. So much was unsure right now, and having an ordinary moment with my friend felt nice. "Please thank Eloise for me."

"We wanted to say how happy we are that you are okay." Chris sat in a chair positioned near the bed.

"Yeah, okay. Well, that is a few days off. Right now, I'm just happy with feeling human," I replied honestly.

"I was told not to ask you anything about it." Chris lifted his eyebrows as if to say that he was asking anyway.

Smiling at my friend, I still avoided his unspoken question. "Yeah, Joseph is going overboard with the protection detail."

"The doctors are worried about you," Chris stated.

"Well, that is because word travels about how I don't stop. Apparently the gossip is I'm a workaholic," I replied sarcastically.

"It looks like you have stopped," he observed.

"Looks are deceiving. I have invoices and other reports under my pillow. Work doesn't stop, and I won't let myself either."

Chris gave me a disapproving look but held his tongue for his own sake. He lived in my home the last time I had the flu with walking pneumonia and witnessed firsthand how, through my illness, my sheer willpower to produce a movie while prepping for my next tour won out. After that, Chris started calling me a machine.

"Stubborn women rule the world," I said to his sideways, judgy look.

Chris was the fourth acting friend to stop by while I recovered, and the small talk wore on me. I could only think of one thing, which stayed on a loop in my head: Who shot me? While I smiled for my visitors and friends, it hung over me—the Sword of Damocles waiting to fall.

After years of cultivating these relationships with people who loved me as I truly loved them, I did my best to be present in the moment for them. But given the circumstances, I struggled to keep up with the pretense.

Chris took his leave after 15 minutes of chit-chat and observing me let out three yawns.

After he departed, I laid in my hospital bed, thinking more and more not allowing the sleep I needed to settle in. One word kept screaming in my mind. It was the only thing that made any sense to me. One word that described why I was lying on my back instead of on a plane heading to Australia to become one more actress to perform Shakespeare's Helena. That one word haunted me.

Family.

As I lay in the hospital, unable to be me—a form of torture—that word was the one thing that kept me on the edge. It was bad enough this was a personal horror. Unable to move at my own pace or free will, forced to allow medical staff help and supervise me as they monitored my healing process. I never fathomed I'd have to endure this treatment.

Family.

The invoices I had "stolen" only took me an hour to complete. I was bored, restless, and hurting. But more than anything else, I was overthinking what happened. The only motive I could think of for my attack was my family—not the one I made, but my blood family.

"Stop being such a grumpy puss," Lydia interrupted my spiraling thought process as she entered the room for a third consecutive visit. I was so happy to see her.

"You know me, Lydia. This rest is killing me," I whined while shuffling around in the bed.

"That is why," Lydia started, reaching into her bag to pull out a small stack of file folders, "I snuck these into you."

"You are a beautiful woman," I said, smiling widely and exhaling my relief.

Lydia crossed over to the hospital bed, "Do you need new pillows? I can have Raylynn get some items from your room."

"Maybe. I'll give that some thought," I said. "I don't want to get too comfortable here."

"Okay," she sighed softly. "So you have the accounting paperwork you need to sign off on here. Then three scripts you need to approve or deny for this week. Finally, you have all the evaluations for upper management."

"Yay, busy work," I grinned, greedily taking the folders from her. "I don't think I've ever been this excited about paperwork."

"I'll try to get your laptop tomorrow," Lydia said slyly.

"This is why you're my favorite," I replied as I held up a hand for a high-five.

Lydia returned the gesture before she sat in the chair next to the bed and we got to work.

We spent the next couple of hours chit-chatting about the paperwork and different aspects of the company, bouncing ideas off one another about the media spin of the current situation. It was going well until we both heard a male voice let out a "Tsk, tsk, tsk" from the door. It was so unexpected that Lydia jumped and I froze; a reflex I wasn't accustomed to.

"Well, well, well," Joseph said, his voice deep and serious as he entered my room.

I looked up to see him smiling and I instantly relaxed, "Do you have a problem?"

"Nope, I just hoped you'd last 24 more hours before you bribed someone to bring you work," he answered, doing his best to sound disappointed. I couldn't help but notice he seemed lighter, maybe because I was finally functioning again.

"No bribing needed this time," I said as Lydia piped up and said, "I got the right offer."

Joseph chuckled, "Okay then, I won't keep you from it. Anything you need from me?"

"Look these reports over." I held up a stack of papers, and he leaned in to take them.

"Second look or final?" he asked.

"Both, since technically I'm out of commission."

The three of us continued to work in the confined space of the hospital room until I attempted to hide a yawn into my arm. Both Joseph and Lydia noticed and let the working conversation end as I slowly fell asleep with the script I was reading in my hands.

Joseph

I kept an eye on Emmeline while I worked, and I noticed she drifted off. I took a deep breath and directed my next words directly to my PR specialist. "Lydia, thank you for bringing her some work," I said softly. "I can see how it helped her relax and gave her something to focus on."

"It was no problem," she chuckled. "She was talking to Alyson Summers when I was here yesterday; like to her broadcast. I knew she was going stir crazy."

"People like her aren't meant to be caged in."

"Nope, we aren't," she agreed.

"On one hand, I wish they could just knock her out so she could rest. But that wouldn't do her any good either."

"No that wouldn't help her. Healing is difficult."

"Yes, that I know," I spoke with such authority that Lydia didn't respond; it was one of the quirks I used to my advantage.

"I just want to know why. Like, you two are my work family. I'm very fond of both of you and to have one of you hurt and not know why? Well, that's killing me," she said, changing the conversation.

"Yes, I know what you mean." The question of why was killing me as well. I had two possible scenarios running around my head, and I hated both versions.

"The police aren't being very forthcoming with me," Lydia said softly. "Though I believe it is because of my job and nothing more."

"Nah, it's not just you," I said, matching her soft tone. "They are keeping their investigation close to their vest with me, too," I paused. "I've been stonewalled."

"That doesn't seem right," Lydia scoffed.

"They have to do their jobs the way they see best. I just need them to catch the shooter; I won't sleep until that happens."

"You can't keep everyone under lock and key," she said with a pointed look. "The others are nervous with the security team present."

"They are a bit much, aren't they?" I pondered, even though I hired the extra security around the office and our home.

"Umm, they are basically a S.W.A.T. team, Joseph," Lydia countered. "Raylynn was terrified of leaving her office, waiting for someone to move wrong and for them to strike."

"Raylynn is a bit skittish to begin with," I laughed as I recalled the first time Emmeline's PA was sent to my office to retrieve files. The girl was a hot mess already, unable to keep up with the work pace. Then she couldn't find a posted note stuck to the backside of her folder to ask for the proper files. Then tripped, landed on my water machine, and dumped 20 gallons onto the carpeted floor.

The poor girl thought she was fired and busted into tears. Still, I laughed it off instead and sent her back with the file Emme had requested via a text, knowing the first-time PA was freaking out.

"Well, working for you two should have punched that out of her by now," Lydia remarked. I attempted to hide my grin, it was funny she said that. During Lydia's first few weeks, she literally said three words—yes, no, mailroom—until she could find her own rhythm in the crazy fast pace and shorthand Emme and I shared. It was something we cultivated over the years of working together. It was no easy task to find how to flow with it.

"I'll have it switched up again. Calm it back down," I mused. "I just am so freaking worried I've gone overboard."

"You always do with her," Lydia confirmed. "It's like," she let her voice trail off as if she was about to say something that wasn't her place to point out, and yet...

I had a gut feeling about the words she was searching for, and frankly, I didn't want to hear it. Giving her a pointed look, I handed her a file to divert her. "This is the projected budget for *Lover's Hand*; please ensure it goes to the proper places. And by the way, it's a stupid title."

"I think it's a working title," Lydia offered.

"Yes, well, that is something we will need to work on."

Lydia took her cue and stood with determination. She was going to say what she was thinking of before anyway. "I've never known the exact definition of your relationship with Emmeline, which has always been a problem," she said matter-of-factly. "But I know you love her. And I've seen the wedding photo, so I know you two *care* greatly for each other. Just... stop freaking out too much on everyone else when it comes to her." She then left, Emme still sleeping soundly.

I laughed softly to myself, thinking about the picture Lydia referred to — the one Emme kept on her desk. It was taken years ago, in another life; with Emme in a wedding dress, me sharp as ever in a tux, and the two of us in a warm embrace on a dance floor. It created so many questions from those who saw it, and we liked to leave them unanswered.

I let Emme sleep and picked up another film's projected budget. The show still had to go on.

Chapter Seven

Emmeline

Sleeping on pain pills was a different type of sleep; one where I never felt completely asleep or rested. My dreams were vivid and wild, enough to make my head spin when I woke up. They also made me not want to fall asleep—it was like entering an alternative universe when I did. The only good spin was it gave me ideas for music. With the steady beeping of the heart monitor, the swoosh of the oxygen machine, and the other constant drips and ticks, my songwriter's heart happily dallied in new melodies and lyrics. Lying in bed, now with access to my laptop, I was creating new things.

"What?" a male voice croaked in surprise. "Who gave you a laptop?"

I smirked, "This is the only good thing about being in this bed. I can write. My music is not suffering due to this unplanned, unarranged, annoying sabbatical," I smarted off to the two visitors who arrived at my room for the first time since the shooting.

"Well, thank God for that. What would the world do if Emmeline's next album was not on time?" Shawn sighed dramatically.

"Don't be an arse," Katy scolded, smacking him lightly as she found a seat next to the window.

"Yeah, Shawn, don't be mean to me," I teased, sounding as snotty as possible. "I could have died. Then how guilty would you have felt for being so mean to me?"

While I meant it as a joke, the room's atmosphere shifted with my words, and I saw the guilt flash through Shawn's face.

"Don't even say that." His response was so serious and out of his typical charming character. "I wouldn't know what I would have done if I'd lost you."

"The news kept talking about how it was touch and go," Katy added.

"Well, as you can see, I'm okay," I told them, attempting to lighten the conversation again. "I'm healing, and the police will catch the shooter. Sooner or later, this will all return to normal."

"Emmes, don't downplay this," Shawn hissed, still standing near the door, afraid to get too close.

"Yeah," Katy jumped in, pulling her legs into her chest. "I did my research. Shootings are serious business. You could have serious complications. You could have had multisystem organ failure. You did have internal bleeding."

"And I'm still at risk for infection and many other scary-sounding issues. But I am a survivor," I interrupted gently, trying to calm them. "And I have an excellent medical team and the love of my family around me."

My friends shared a look that told me they had discussed this in more detail than I thought they would. It also told me they wouldn't press me, but I worried they might decide to press Joe, whenever he came back from the meeting I wouldn't let him miss.

The three of us had been together a long time—they were some of the first people I connected with when I showed up in the City of Dreams to pursue my path. Even if our relationship was not normal or based on complete truths, I had to try. I met the pair when I was passing as a 17-year-old and experiencing what I said was a horrible breakup. The three of us were co-starring in my first project, *On Point*. Katy and Shawn provided me with a refuge Joe wasn't able to give. A distraction from the emotional pain Joe and I were living in.

I hardly spoke to anyone on that first day of filming. At my audition, I presented as a confident young lady who was made for the role, but that day my nerves got the best of me.

"Where are you at, Emmeline?" Katy asked, bringing me out of my thoughts and back into the hospital room.

I knew I wasn't fooling them, but I wasn't fooling myself either on this one. The more time passed without the shooter being found, the more I had convinced myself my attack was more terrible than anyone could imagine. That everything in my life was now irrevocably changed. And when it all came out, people like Katy and Shawn would be out of my life. Not because they wouldn't love or care for me anymore, but rather for their own good.

"Just thinking about the first day I met you two and how you became my best friend," I replied easily, giving her a smile.

"You mean the day the producers realized that just because your toes pointed the right way didn't mean you could act?" Shawn said, a grin returning to his face.

"Yeah, and when you and Katy decided we needed to go bar hopping," I added to the retelling.

"No, we went dancing at a club, and you had a meltdown," Katy interjected.

That part was true; the acting was hard for me, and I couldn't fake a lifetime of friendship, but the dancing was easy. The movie, *On Pointe,* chronicled the first year of a dancer's life in her new company. So Katy planned a night out for us to mesh together so the screen time would be a reflection of life.

Joe had been off somewhere, doing God knows what to secure us the means we needed to start our company. We decided our direction at that point and needed to get started. But I found it hard to resist Katy's invitation for the night out.

"I'd never seen a girl cry like that on the dance floor," Katy pointed out.

"Yeah, but you rushed me off the floor so fast. You were so panicked," I chuckled.

It was the first night in forever that I had been able to let go of control and I couldn't help but cry happy tears from the freedom of it all.

"I thought you had been abused," Katy recalled.

"No, it was just … It was the freedom of it," I confessed. "It was the first time I could act without thought."

"We have been besties ever since."

"I wouldn't have had it any other way."

Suddenly, the tension was gone and we found ourselves talking about our friendship over the years. The way Katy and Shawn tag-teamed the retellings had me giggling, but with each laugh, my belly throbbed. Shawn was being ridiculous and trying to make me smile, while Katy recalled stories starting with "One time when…"

Eventually, Joe came back from his meeting and joined in with the giggles. He reminded us all about Shawn's bright idea of making a suit out of duct tape and artificial turf for an event that supported the Angel Wings charity. Then he saw me wince, and went mute, watching me for any more signs of distress.

When he saw enough, Joe reached over and hit the button on my pain pump and though I should have been mad, I was so grateful I felt sleep coming on. I missed the end of the story about a fashion show where I had to put three stitches into Katy's leg as I drifted off.

Joseph

"Now that she's asleep, you two can tell me what everyone is saying since I'm not in the group text right now," I confronted them, needing all the details.

"No, you can tell us what happened," Katy demanded. She stood up, moved around to stand at the foot of the hospital bed, and placed her hand on her hip showing me she meant business.

"How'd you let this happen?" Shawn asked, his tone full of accusation.

"*Let?*" I repeated. "What do you mean 'Let this happen'?" I snarled.

My eyes volleyed between Katy and Shawn waiting to see who would throw it out there.

"There has always been more than meets the eye between you two," Shawn levied. "And you protect her like a Bishop protects the Queen in a chess game. But she was shot on your watch. This happened to her when you should have been protecting her."

I was doing my best to keep my temper at bay when Shawn pushed further by towering over me as I sat next to Emmeline's bed. "What mistake did you make?" he asked darkly.

"Sit down now," I warned, my fist clenching the arm of the chair.

"What Shawn means to say..." Katy started, sensing the anger rising.

"Oh, I understand what he meant clearly," I barked. "But if he doesn't sit down in the next 30 seconds, I'll make him sit down."

Katy gave a pleading look to Shawn as I swiftly stood and made a point to tower over the actor now.

"You have no idea who you are dealing with," I said coldly, surprising myself even. "You have no idea what I will do if you don't back off."

Shawn backed off and cowardly put the hospital bed and Katy between the two of us. "We just care about her." His voice had significantly lowered, no longer powered by anger and accusations.

"Do you think I don't know?" I countered him.

My two friends look dumbfounded. "I've loved this girl since she was born. She is my best friend, my other half. She's a *queen* to me!" I shouted.

I couldn't read the look on either of their faces as I brought my tone dangerously low, "Everything I do is for her."

My arms were shaking and my hands balled into fists at my sides. Mentally, I was gearing up for a fight and these two were close to setting me off. I had to get my temper under control before I did something Emmeline would hate me for.

"Please calm down," Katy squeaked out.

I had buried my rage so far and they were the unfortunate souls who let the gate open, so I continued. "You come in here, reminisce about the past, then wait until she's asleep to accuse me? As if I haven't been there every time for her? That won't fly."

Shawn stammered, "I'm sorry."

"You think you love her? You think you want to be with her? You've stuck around all this time as the friend to give yourself a chance," I spat at Shawn as I sat back down. I did not want to scare my friends, but they had poked a raw nerve and they would have to hear what I had to say. "That won't happen, Shawn. Especially if you come against me. Visiting hours are over now. Goodbye."

"I'm sorry, Joseph, I didn't think about what you were going through," Katy said, leaning down and kissing Emmeline goodbye on the forehead.

"Just find out what happened to her," Shawn said, quickly scurrying to the door and keeping as much distance between us as the small room provided.

I tried to take a few deep breaths, teetering on an edge I hadn't been on in a long time. I couldn't help but feel like the young man with temper issues again. It was as if I had been a sleeping bear, and with everything that had happened to Emmeline, with everyone questioning and people attempting to pry deeper than ever before, my rage was making itself known. My head hung forward as I tried to reign myself in.

"He happened to her."

The voice that interrupted the quiet of the room was all too familiar. My head popped up to meet gazes with the man in the doorway and I knew my disbelief clouded my features. "You can't be here."

After kicking Katy and Shawn out, I was jonesing for a cigarette to calm back down; seeing him was enough to push me over the edge. I needed time to take the edge off before I dealt with him.

"I need to be here," the man responded coolly. I gave him a once over and saw he was wearing a gray three-piece suit with a corresponding blue collared shirt. He looked very sharp and put together, but panic and fear illuminated his face.

"Seriously, you can't be here," I reiterated, standing and meeting him in the doorway, using my body to block him from stepping any closer to the sleeping Emmeline.

"I have to see her." His voice was pleading and sad. "I have to know she's okay."

The look on his face was enough to make me struggle with the decision. I wanted to let him in; his desperation and fear spoke volumes. The fact he had shown up said even more. And I understood it all too well, but he wasn't supposed to be here. His presence would cause so many problems–problems we couldn't handle at the moment. I didn't want to let him close to Emme. The meds knocked her out so deeply she would never know, but I wondered how fair this situation was to her. Her life was already upside down, and now *he* was here.

"Please..." His voice broke, his eyes downcast to his shoes. I just couldn't turn him away.

"She will be out for about three hours," I said quietly.

"Is that code for 'Be gone by then'?" he responded.

"Yes," I said as firmly as I could.

After a moment's pause, I hugged the man and felt relief flood through my system. He was here. That was bad, but I was glad to see him all the same. I muttered that I'd be back before leaving the room to let him have a few moments with her. For good measure, I shut the door.

"Ethan, make sure no one interrupts them, not even hospital personnel," I instructed the security guard at the door. "I want him followed when he leaves, then never allow him here again."

When Ethan nodded his understanding, masking his confusion of my absolute trust in an apparent stranger, I disappeared down the hall so I could find a cigarette. It was a habit I'd kicked a long time again, but I could no longer ignore the need for the relief it provided me.

I could only imagine what he was doing, *saying* to Emme as he sat by her side. Most likely, he was apologizing for her injury. Probably promising her he would make the culprit pay. I knew he wouldn't be able to stand not touching her—he probably already snuggled up next to her. I could only hope she was relaxed, knowing she was safe. I knew him well enough to know he would just sit and talk; silence was never his strong suit.

Once outside in the hospital gardens, I pulled a cigarette from the pack crammed in my pocket. I lit it and inhaled deeply, attempting to calm down. Smoking on the grounds may be prohibited, but there was no one around to scold me about it.

Shawn's accusations earlier left me raw. I already felt guilty and had beat myself up over all this, but to have friends saying the same? It burned. But now *he* was here, it was possible he could enlighten me on the murky details and take some of the stress away.

The Walking Dead tone on my cell phone jingled, "Joe's phone," I answered.

"Look, I am calling you because ... well, quite frankly, I have no other options," Emme's brother rushed out.

I blew out smoke with my heavy breath, "I thought I said you shouldn't be calling."

"I know he's there," the gruff voice responded. "Just confirm it."

"You know who's here?" I countered. If anything, I was going to have fun with her brother. It would bring me the smallest amount of joy in this crap fest.

"Joseph, just tell me," he swore softly. "Just please let me know he came on his own before war falls down on us all."

"What are you talking about? War falling down on us? Did you swallow a weird language book?"

"No, things are just," he stammered. "Is he there? I just need a yes or no."

"What's going on?" Now I was scared. If all this crazy talk threatened Emmeline, he needed to tell me.

"Things are changing in this camp."

The vagueness of it all was tiring. "How so?

"I don't know," he stuttered.

"You should know," I said forcefully, my calm disappearing. My face was hot and my shoulders tensed back up around my neck.

"It doesn't matter what I should or shouldn't know," he snapped back.

"Tell me what is happening now," I demanded.

"I'm not allowed to, you know that. Where is he?"

"Jackson, what changed?" I demanded again, louder.

"My sister was shot! It caused chaos amongst the families and now that he's done... he can't break the rules right now."

"Seems like all the rules are being broken now. Tell me who shot her."

"It doesn't matter right now," he rushed out.

"What!?" I lost it completely. My fist balled up— how could anything be more important than Emmeline? "Then what matters right now?"

"The King is AWOL, and I must find him before the kingdom falls."

"You'll find him soon. I'm sure of it," I barked, then slammed my phone on the ground out of anger, watching it break into pieces.

Another long breath left me. "Great. Now I'll have to replace that phone."

If Jackson wasn't going to talk to me, the man currently standing next to Emmeline's bed would.

Chapter Eight

Joseph

Lingering in the garden was no longer an option. I hotboxed a second cigarette in a few minutes then returned to Emme's room. I knew my day was nowhere close to over. When I turned the corner, a fuming Lydia waited for me.

"Why won't Ethan let me in?" Lydia demanded curtly.

"I told him she needed some rest," I answered smoothly. "Deal with it."

"I tried calling you," she stated, her eyes rolling over me, nose wrinkling as she smelt the smoke on me.

"My phone broke. Will you get Maddi to get a replacement?"

"I'm not your assistant," she snapped. "You get in touch with her."

This was the day that kept on giving. She was downright livid, and I would have to deal with this sooner rather than later.

"What has gotten you so ruffled?" I shook my head, knowing I wasn't ready for another confrontation. No high in the world could keep me calm from all the confrontations I'd already had and the one with the man in the room with Emme right now. Lydia needed to be placated.

I could see she was currently attempting to read me to see how far she should push this, but her anger was getting the best of her.

"Ethan is NEVER to keep me away from her."

"That's not your call to make," I replied simply.

"She's my boss, my best friend, and I need access to her," Lydia pressed again.

We were both attempting to keep anger at bay, so I laughed. Laughed at her anger, the day, this whole stupid mess...

"In other words," I started. "You don't like being told no."

"Why do you do that?" Lydia asked. Her anger seemed to ease with my laughter.

"It needed to be done. Give me 10 minutes, then you can bug her." I wasn't going to engage her further; I continued into Emme's room to find Ethan standing firmly in place with a bright red face.

"What happened to you?"

"Lydia," he grumbled.

"What?" I questioned, confused.

"Wouldn't let her pass. She slapped my face more than once," Ethan reported, his annoyance not even bleeding into his tone. I wasn't sure how he could remain so professional.

I sighed heavily. "Good job. Stand down now. I've got the guard for a few minutes. Get some ice."

I relied on Ethan, and he impressed me time and time again. But standing up against Lydia and still living to tell the tale was enough to know he would continue to be Emme's bodyguard. I kept him close to see if I still trusted him. I wasn't sure he would still have a job when this was over, but he had just changed my mind. Lydia was one to almost always get her way; Ethan stopping her was a good mark in his favor.

"You are making him leave?" he asked.

"Yes. You have someone ready to tail him?"

"Affirmative," he confirmed. "The only question is how long?"

"I want to know where he goes—hotel, airport, train, wherever."

"Understood," Ethan gave a short head nod.

I watched Ethan head down the hall and retrieve his phone from a pocket, making final arrangements for the tail. I steadied myself as I entered the room. The first thing I saw was the man lying beside Emmeline, her head tucked against his chest. The sight made me regret what I was about to do. In a lame attempt to allow him more time, I walked over to Emme's phone, entered her passcode, and found the contact I needed.

"Maddi, yeah hi," I started when the call connected. "My phone is broken. You can call me on Emme's phone if you need me. And if you could arrange to get me a new phone, I'd appreciate it," I mumbled to my personal assistant's voicemail.

The standard hospital room size had been okay for most of this stay, but at this moment, it felt like a tiny Tic-Tac box.

"How'd you break your phone?" he asked with a knowing chuckle.

"I just did."

"I bet you threw it against a wall," he speculated. "Like you used to.."

"Well if I did," I huffed, "It's your fault."

"Zero contact, not so zero," he mused.

"It could have never been zero contact. Information had to be exchanged. How long have you known?"

"Always suspected," he confirmed. "Choose to not know."

"Well, that is why my phone is broken. Jackson called me. And he said that 'The kingdom is crumbling.'"

"I didn't exactly plan my trip," he sighed, accepting the message and understanding its meaning. It was obvious to me what Jackson had meant. This trip was causing the Table to act out. "I watched the news, saw the headline break, and without a second thought I headed to the jet."

"She was hurt; you acted," I said dryly, understanding his action and process.

"Just like you did. I talked to Dr. Drake. He says your actions gave her the fighting chance she needed."

"Really gotta love those HIPPA laws; they do nothing," I snarked.

"Money talks," he said dryly.

"Yeah, I thought I'd taken care of talking with my money."

"Well, I have a few other tricks."

"Obviously." When he didn't respond, I stood there like an idiot at the foot of her hospital bed waiting for my convictions to return.

"You need to tell me if this was my fault or yours," I said sharply but quietly.

"Can't be yours. You have done everything we agreed to," he replied solemnly, accepting the blame.

"I still need to know who made the call and who acted upon it."

"We both know who it was," he said sternly. "We just need to know why now—and why that jackal felt he could."

"And what you will do about it," I added firmly.

He nodded his head, and his grip tightened around Emme, who was still sleeping soundly, but I wasn't sure for how much longer.

"You have to leave," I said very solemnly.

"Yes, I know." The accepting tone in his voice told me he wasn't going to be a problem.

"She's okay. I'll keep her safe," I said, reassuring him I would continue to do what I had always done.

"Thanks to you."

"It was our deal," I said dryly.

"Brother, I owe you a debt I can never repay," the man replied before kissing Emmeline on her temple and standing up.

"Same, Brother. It's the same here." I suddenly felt even more emotional than before. "Because of you, I have an extraordinary life. One that has been phenomenal."

"You talk like it's over." He stood, adjusting his suit back to a pristine state.

I shrugged, "Just a gut feeling."

"I've had the same one. That everything is blown up now."

We both shared a knowing look. "I'll have Jackson tell you all I can when I know it."

"Thanks. I know that isn't what is supposed to happen." I didn't say the part both of us were thinking. He should have never taken an attempt on Emme's life either.

"Goodbye, darling," he whispered. Then looking back at me, the man in the suit left the hospital room without a fight and was followed by one of LJ's private security guards. I was told later he went straight to the airport and boarded a waiting private jet. I hoped he would take me at my word and that seeing her was enough to keep him at bay.

"Today has been rough," I told Emmeline as if she was awake and listening. I was ready to collapse as Lydia came barreling into the room, ready for a fight.

"What is happening here?" Her voice was soft, but her tone was sharp. She was heated, and apparently, it was time to have this out.

"Happening with what?" I didn't want to deal with this now. I didn't want to lie to Lydia for another moment. I wanted to run, straighten out my head, and find some peace.

"You are keeping secrets and telling lies, both of which do not bode well for us, this brand, or this company. And they sure don't bode well for me."

Emmeline was starting to stir, probably hearing more of this conversation than she would later admit.

"Yes, Lydia, there are. But..."

"But nothing," she interrupted. "How am I supposed to deal with the PR matters if you don't give me the full picture?"

"Because those details don't matter."

"That phone call the other day seemed to matter."

"Right now is when you choose to lose it on me?"

"Yes, I demand an explanation." Lydia stood with her arms crossed, her body ramrodded straight and radiating anger.

"Lydia, I just kicked Katy and Shawn out because they accused me of failing her and blamed me for this. I have people crawling out of the woodwork trying to see her. I have to have the security of everyone as a priority. We are all stressed because someone just tried to *kill* her. Can we please just slow this train down for two bloody minutes?"

While I was aggressive with Lydia, it was nothing like I'd been with Shawn. It was still enough to show her I was not dealing with this right now.

"I'm sorry, sir," she said quickly and softly. "I think the stress is getting to me too."

"It's been a rough few days," I sighed, sinking into a chair. "I have a feeling it will get worse before it gets better."

Her face screamed that she wanted to ask more questions.

"Lydia, I promise we will talk soon."

Nodding her head, she kept her mouth shut as Emmeline woke up and sighed heavily.

Emmeline

I wanted to be home ever since I first woke up in the ICU. At the time, Joe and the medical staff made me completely aware of how impossible that would be. I didn't protest because I knew they were right. I wasn't doing well when I first woke up. Now, I felt like I may be ready—and I was hooked up to less equipment than before. I needed to process, to feel safe, and to take a beat to recalculate. None of that felt possible under the constant eye of everyone. I needed to go home.

Once LJ Productions did well enough for us to be successful in the world of production, Joesph and I built our first home. I poured myself into the architecture, making it a home I could host in, but more importantly, a place I could recharge in. Specifically, my bedroom that was on the third floor.

It housed a large king-sized poster bed, oversized reading chair, walk-in closet, beautiful white furniture, a private covered porch, cream-painted walls, and blue trims. I created a haven for myself and I needed that space now. I wouldn't be able to fully recover anywhere else. The hospital was busy, with constant noise. People are always in and out of the room. The physical exams seemed endless and there was no privacy whatsoever.

I opened my eyes and saw Lydia and Joseph were in a standoff of wills over something I could only assume was not good. So I needed to change the subject. "I want to go home," I mumbled softly.

"What do you want?" Joseph asked me, so lost in his standoff with Lydia he didn't hear me.

"I want to go home," I said again, my voice stronger, louder.

"Emme," Lydia started, "You shouldn't push yourself."

"Joe, I want to go home," I pleaded again. "I want my bed, not this cot. We both know you are delaying my discharge. Please."

He sighed heavily and I knew he wouldn't deny me this request. "Okay, I'll talk to the doctors."

He was going crazy here too. He couldn't be in control, hence the number of security guards and extra protection everywhere he could get them. He left the room to discuss my discharge, and Lydia stepped out to answer a call. My abdomen was throbbing with pain for the first time since the shooting. Joseph had been doing all he could to keep me numb—it was his way of protecting me. But I needed the pain.

I took advantage of being alone and worked my way into a sitting position, then pushed myself to stand up. I had only been out of bed a handful of times, and always with the aid of a nurse or medical student. It took more energy than I would have thought. Then took a few steps to the bathroom. I pulled the gown up and peeled the tape and bandage.

I vividly remember how the force of the bullet pushed my body backward and how the pain echoed through my being. When I looked down to see the blood, not knowing what was happening, my hand lingered in it, like a child would in finger paint. It all happened so fast and yet slow at the same time. When I hit the ground, my whole body ached. Standing in the hospital bathroom, I could see it all playing back.

But now it was different. The pain from an emergency operation, needle sticks, and lying prone for so long made my body hurt in a whole new way. And I was so afraid it would take forever until I found myself again.

My gaze lingered over the wound. It was the first time I saw my flesh stitched back together, discolored, and jagged. The imperfections of it were such a contrast to how it previously looked. I vainly wondered if it would ever be as pretty as it had been. What additional surgeries would result from this one?

"Emme," Lydia called, entering the room.

"In here," I called back, trying to save her from panic.

She quickly came to the bathroom and froze. Her eyes landed on my abdomen.

"Oh," Lydia whispered. "I..."

"It's gross, I know," I said, dismissing her reaction and trying to keep both of us from having a huge emotional breakdown. Even if I did deserve one.

"It's real now," she whimpered.

"Yeah," I whispered back. "I was shot." The physical evidence was no longer hidden.

I looked up at her and could read the variety of emotions flickering across her face. I was sure my reflection mirrored those emotions.

"Let's get you home," Joseph interrupted. He silently slipped into the room and joined us in examining the wound. His face was unreadable but he was struggling like I was.

It felt like all the stress, fear, and reaction boiled down to this moment. We were looking at the product of someone's attempt on my life, and it hurt. There was no pretending, no way around it. My life hung in the balance and somehow I survived. Now I had to recover and move forward.

Chapter Nine

Emmeline

Dressing in the sweats and T-shirt Lydia brought me, there was a soft knock on the door.

"That's probably Jake with your discharge paperwork," Lydia said as she rounded the bed to open the door.

I started to pull at my shirt to make myself more decent than I had been since I woke up.

"Emme," she paused, looking over her shoulder to me, "You up to answering questions?"

As I glanced up, a very angry man wearing a cheap looking suit was standing in the doorway. Clearly this man was from some law agency; you could see how important he was trying to make himself seem. Ethan was behind him, clearly been given a stand down command, and was frustrated by it.

"For?" I asked with a soft tone. I hadn't mentally prepared myself for when local law enforcement would make their way to interview me about the incident.

"The Franklin County Police Department," the stranger confirmed his agency.

Lydia exited without saying anything, but I hoped she was on her way to find Joe; I didn't want to do this part alone.

"I wondered when I'd see an officer," I muttered, mostly to myself.

"It's Detective, actually," he corrected. "Detective Adrian Sawyer. I've been investigating your attempted murder."

"Well, what can you tell me?" I sat at the foot of the hospital cot, which they had the nerve to call a bed, and started focusing on the facts I knew. I had been very aware of the security protocols and work that went into keeping me safe on a theoretical level, Joseph kept a handle on that, so I didn't know how much help I would be to the detective. Nor did I know whatever Joseph had been keeping from me, he clearly knew things I didn't yet, leaving me unsure how much I should help any agency.

"What can you tell us, Detective?" Joseph reiterated, entering the room and sitting in his chair.

"Mr. MacDonald, thank you for joining us," Sawyer responded, his voice was authoritative, he wanted us to know he was directing this conversation. He moved to the window on the far side of the room, turning to look at us both directly.

"Of course, Detective, I've been anxiously awaiting your findings," Joseph said, using his COO voice–an air of authority, but respectfulness, waiting on what he would say and do.

"Here is what we have determined after speaking with stadium personnel, reviewing hours of CCV footage, reviewing personnel files, and interviewing all possible witnesses," Detective Sawyer flipped open the packet of materials in his hands. n. "The culprit went to great lengths to deceive everyone. He was hired as a janitor with the aid of a rather convincing alias, including all the appropriate documentation."

While reading the file, I could see that he was clearly watching me and my reaction to all the new information, he knew that math was not adding up for my life, and was trying to deduce what I was keeping to myself.

"Using a medically documented injury, we think he slowly brought all the needed pieces to build a rifle at the stadium. This tells us he had a well-thought-out, planned attack against you. If this person was hired to murder you, we believe he was contracted well over two years ago." He remained standing near the window, instead of sitting down to be on the same level as us. He didn't trust me, I wouldn't trust him.

"Why would someone want to hire someone to kill Emme?" Joseph asked as panic began to creep across my body, forcing me to take a very deep, painful breath. Joseph was also investigating, but he had to do so from the point of view of the victim.

"That's what we are unsure about," the Detective said. " Many times when a stalker wants to hurt their obsession, there are warning signs before he escalates. Based on all the information we have now, there has been no indication that Ms. Jones was being stalked or in any danger for that matter. "

"Until I was," I whispered, my hand resting on my abdomen as I fought the urge to lay back and give my body rest.

"Do you know why anyone would want to harm you?" Detective Sawyer asked me directly, his mistrusting eyes keeping me in his focus.

My eyes volleyed to Joe; I needed him to answer this one. My mind started racing and running through all the scenarios I could fathom. None of them were ones I felt like sharing with a detective.

"She's a celebrity; there are those out there who do seek to harm her," Joseph answered matter-of-factly. "It's part of the job, unfortunately."

He kicked back in the chair he'd been living in, giving an air of finality to his explanation. I could tell he was guarded, keeping truth from the detective and me, I had to figure it out.

"Yes, but I don't have any reason to believe that angle applies here given the measures the perp took," Detective Sawyer flipped through the pages of his folder as he scanned over the data. It was a tactic I knew well; he was still investigating, and his focus now was getting out of me what he obviously believed I was keeping from him. "The extreme measures of this attack indicate it was personal. The fact this shooter took time to plan each and every detail and *not* kill you leads us to believe the person or persons behind the hit wanted to send you a message." Detective Sawyer stopped and again made eye contact with me. "I'll ask you again Ms. Jones, is there anyone you know who could have orchestrated such an attack against you?"

I looked to Joe, whose face was still unreadable, his poker face in full effect. For me, the information Detective Sawyer provided allowed the pieces to finally click into place. I no longer had a feeling about who could have done this—I knew there was only one answer. Whether he realized it or not, Detective Sawyer had shared far more with me than I could ever give him in return. Hearing how seamlessly this shooter acted told me more as well. The Family had planned and executed this. The organization I thought I had kept at bay for all these years had shown they could always reach me. The only question I had now was what was the intent?

"What was the janitor's alias?" I asked, hoping my voice didn't give away my newfound realization, the name would confirm my suspicion.

Detective Sawyer flipped a few pages in the file folder, read the name to himself, and then looked back to me, "Mitchell Haynes."

"It sounds familiar, but it doesn't mean anything to me," I replied as smoothly as I could. In fact, I knew that surname well. I pulled from my acting box and put on a face; Detective Sawyer couldn't know how well I knew that name.

"Ms. Jones, is there anything you can think of that could aid us? Anything that could indicate why you would be targeted on such a personal level?" the Detective asked.

"Detective Sawyer, I can't think of any reason someone would want to hurt me," I replied, working hard to make it sound as natural as possible. "I run a production company and occasionally sing and act. I operate a nonprofit in my spare time to help people. I work hard. None of what has happened makes any sense to me." As I finished, I found myself thankful I did not still have a heart monitor on; my erratic heartbeat would given me away.

Detective Sawyer stared at me for a beat, his face blank but his eyes alluding to the fact he still did not trust me and a part of him, no matter how good of an actor I was, didn't believe me. "One more question," he said after a moment, flipping through more papers in his folder before he grasped a small item. "Does this man look familiar?" he asked, handing me a printed photo from a security camera. "The arena has cameras in places staff members are unaware of, as a form of theft prevention. They are not even listed on blueprints and were installed to be unnoticeable. So the alleged shooter wasn't aware of them. We were able to grab a usable photograph from the footage."

Holding the photo in my hand, knowing Detective Sawyer's eyes were boring into me as I stared at the image, I knew I could not give away that I recognized the man immediately. It didn't matter how many years had passed, the wrinkles now on his face, the grays sticking out from his ballcap, I knew the man who had attempted to take my life. The truth was, he'd spent my whole life trying to pull off my murder.

I wanted to panic. There was no doubt now—every suspicion I had was confirmed by this photo. It was him. It was The Family. My stomach flipped on its own accord, and I wondered if my body could handle me vomiting.

I passed Joe the still frame. I had to remain neutral; I couldn't drop my act now. I couldn't admit to knowing him. If I did, it would all come out—my history, background, and deeply buried past. Everything I was duty-bound to keep a secret.

I could feel Detective Sawyer watching me, so I looked at Joseph and shrugged, allowing my body language to speak for me. Let it say if this man shot me, who he is, why would he do that.

"What evidence is there that suggests this person is the culprit?" Joe asked, pulling Detective Sawyer's attention away from me after a quick glance at the photo.

Joe's life and mine had always been entangled. He knew the man in the photo just as well as I did. He couldn't have any doubt he was the one who pulled the trigger.

"We have footage of him entering the crow's nest near a lighting house where the shot originated," his voice lacked the authority it had started with, he no longer was the man in charge in this room. "There's significant evidence of an individual being up there. We can track that individual's movement from the moment he was hired at the arena to the night of the shooting. After the shooting, however, he disappears and never returns. So that itself is suspicious."

"What leads do you have to capture him?" Joseph said, sounding all business.

My eyes watched the detective, he was already out of options, I was his last resort for him. Since I wasn't helping aid his investigation; it would go cold. This would be a loss for him professionally, and due to my cultural status, I was sure that would impact his career negatively.

"Unfortunately, none," the Detective replied. "I needed to see if you could identify this man as he is officially a person of interest. None of our facial recognition software has been able to identify him."

"I'm sorry," I said softly. "I want him captured and prosecuted. I need closure."

"Yes, of course," Detective Sawyer replied. He obviously was disappointed and doing his best not to show it.

"Sir, Emmeline has just been discharged. She needs to rest. Is there anything further?" Joseph asked, pressing hard to close the conversation.

"No, Mr. MacDonald. I just need to confirm some personal information," Detective Sawyer replied.

Joe stood up, speaking loud enough for those in the hallway to hear, "Lydia, would you please answer Detective Sawyer's questions so I can get Emme home?"

The door opened immediately as if they had planned this to happen, and Lydia stood in the doorway, "Of course, Joseph," she replied.

With that, Joe guided the Detective out of my room and into Lydia's care before he was back and working on getting me discharged. In a very short time, I found myself in a wheelchair, being pushed through more hallways than I knew existed in this place as Ethan guided us to a waiting SUV. The goal was to get me home without any paparazzi or reporters hounding us at the door. But right now, I could only focus on the fact I had held a photo of the man who shot me—and I knew who I was looking at.

"Let me walk out to the car and see if there are any lurkers," Ethan said as we reached the door. "I'll come back and grab you if the coast is clear."

"Thanks," I whispered.

That was all I needed right now—paparazzi shots of me leaving the hospital in my sweats. It would just add to the whole circus of my life.

I watched him as Ethan walked to the car. He was the best bodyguard I had over the last year, his whole demeanor screamed American hero. His classic look made him quite the ladies' man in the office and on tour. In another life, I might have been interested in him. But all I would ever allow myself now was to look. I had no romantic life before this and would not seek one now.

"Coast seems clear, Ms. Jones," he said on his return. He was gentle with his movement as he wheeled me toward Joe's SUV.

"Thanks, Ethan," I said.

The door popped open as I got closer, and Joe climbed out.

Reaching for his hand, I attempted to pull myself up.

"Now, would you be patient?" Joe scolded me.

"You are lucky I took the wheels."

"If you didn't, we'd still be waiting for you to arrive."

Between some more crap talk, he got me in the car with very little jostling. My whole body hurt, there was no hiding that, but going home would be worth the pain.

"Who's driving?" I asked, looking at Joe as he started to shut the door.

"This ride will just be us. I'm driving."

"Oh," I said, swallowing back the pain my body felt.

He circled the car and climbed into the driver's seat. I had the second row to myself and stretched my limbs to find a comfortable spot, not even bothering to buckle up. I didn't think the pressure would be something I could handle.

"Thanks," I whispered to him as he started the SUV. He wanted me to stay in the hospital since I was easier to control there. He could have medical staff checking in on me with the slightest whimper. Staying there would be the easiest way to keep me healthy and healing fast. But I appreciated that he understood I had to get out. .

"Don't bust your stitches or we will be right back." His tone was light, but I knew it was more than a joking statement. He would rush me back at the slightest sign of distress.

"What do we do now?" I asked. He pulled out of the hospital parking lot, a sedan with Ethan and Lydia following behind us.

"I'm still thinking about that."

I watched his profile—jaw set, eyes forward. He was processing all of this just as I was. And he was fuming.

"No one is safe around me now," I sighed.

"No one ever really was," he retorted, a little brutishly.

"It felt safe," I murmured. "At least for a while."

"When I see him...," Joe started, his words tapering off.

"I know. I know what will need to be done." My thoughts hadn't veered in those directions in quite some time. But here I was, my old life coming back so quickly, I was falling into old habits—just like riding a bicycle. There would have to be a reckoning and repercussions for the attempt on my life. The Table would see to it, and if not them, Joseph "No One Hurts My Family" MacDonald would.

Joe drove through the city like a professional, weaving in and out of traffic but also trying his best to not cause me any more pain. We were at a lull in the conversation, even though there was much more to say. I just wasn't sure how.

"Emme, don't be afraid," Joe said firmly. "I'll keep you safe."

"I'm not afraid. I'm just..." Now I tapered off, struggling to say what I wanted.

"You're at a loss for words," he joked ruefully. "Shocking."

"Jerk."

"I still have your back," Joe said, his tone softening.

"I'll always have yours," I swore in allegiance to him.

Joseph finally turned the car down a one-lane private drive; our home sat a mile and a half back, and I had never been more grateful to see it.

"Is everyone we know here?" I asked, seeing all the cars parked. A sight that would have typically filled me with joy. Now all I felt was dread.

"Probably," he said dryly.

"Oh," I whimpered.

"Look, I have been quite intentional with my security placement. There was a list of who was and wasn't allowed to visit the hospital. Which means there are a lot of people who have been missing you. I guess Lydia let the beans spill. But I will make them all leave if that is what you want," Joe stated. I could read it in his eyes—he would scorch the Earth for me if I asked. "I'm comfortable being the bad guy right now."

"No, let them stay," I sighed. "But I may have to disappear for a while."

"Just let me know, and we will sweep you out of the living room," he promised.

"I just don't know how much longer I can keep my composure," I said, meeting his gaze in the rearview mirror.

He nodded in acknowledgment.

"Joseph ... Thomas shot me." I twisted my head in an attempt to hide the emotions that now painted my face at the admission.

Joseph

Emmeline steeled herself against the turmoil stirring inside her and put her business-as-usual face on as I parked in front of the house. People called her a robot, but she was that way for a reason. How she could box in a subject and accomplish a task was astonishing for those not used to that sort of behavior.

"Don't help me too much out of the car," Emmeline whispered. "I need to start standing on my own, literally."

"I have your back," I replied. "Remember that means not letting you do stupid things."

"Yes, I know that, but this isn't stupid," she protested.

"Take the day you are released from the hospital to let everyone take care of you."

She grunted something to me as I exited the vehicle. I had to chuckle as I went to open her door.

"Emme, I know this is a lot," I said, trying to temper her annoyance. "I can kick everyone out, and we can process it together."

"No." Her tone was firm as she spoke. "It's in the box. Let's go visit with our family and friends."

I picked her tiny frame up, even though she protested, and carried her to the house. There was no reason for her to walk the distance with her injuries still fresh. It would wear her out, and she would sleep during the entire visit.

The whole house was noisy when I opened the door. The main entrance was on the second floor, where all the common areas were, so I was able to carry Emme to a sofa easily and gently let her settle in. I wanted to help her adjust but her look of determination was enough to know she had it. After she assured me she was fine, I went off to find our guests.

Opening the pocket doors to the dining room, I came face-to-face with all our friends at the table, having a meal.

"Joseph!" Katy squealed, her hands hitting the wooden table. "Is she here?"

"Be easy, she's in the living room," I replied before taking my seat at the head of the table. It was just so nice to be back home.

I watched Katy leap up and head to the living room, where I heard her squeal again. As I sat, a plate appeared before me, compliments of Lydia. I couldn't help but smile—she still loved me too.

Losing myself in the rhythm of the noise, and the chaos of our lives was easy, but I couldn't ignore that the normalcy of it was gone. I had to process what Detective Sawyer had shared with us, do so quickly, and not let it cross my face. Hearing the giggles from the living room and the chatter around me in the dining room was familiar yet somehow strange. The tension of the events that led us here felt like a weight. I wasn't sure if it was just me or if the whole room was feeling the strain.

"Hey man," a voice from where Katy had previously been, broke through my thoughts. I clenched my jaw; I wasn't sure if I could stomach Shawn today unless his attitude changed. I had too much on my mind.

"Yes?" I asked, taking a bit of the meal Lydia had given me.

"I just wanted to apologize for that day in the hospital," Shawn said sheepishly. "I was wrong, so wrong."

"You were," I agreed plainly.

"I'm just sorry," he continued. "You were right. There were so many things I was feeling, I should have handled it all differently." Shawn was stumbling over his words, spewing word vomit all over the place. I had completely forgotten how angry he made me that day or how badly I intimidated him before throwing him out of Emme's room. There were bigger problems than a Chad actor who wanted to throw weight around.

I raised my hand to stop him, "It's good. We were all stressed that day."

At that, he visibly relaxed "I just...," he started after a moment.

"I know," I interrupted. "It was a bad day, but we're good."

Shawn took the win and went to find Emme along with half the table. I couldn't hear any of the conversations, but I knew Emme was covered in the love of her made-family.

Dropping my head to look at my plate, I decided to dig into the meatloaf and eat my first non-vending machine meal in days, quietly absorbing the sounds of the chatter around me. There was much deal with, but for now, I'd take this comfort of being at home.

Chapter Ten

Joseph

Retreating to the private porch just off her bedroom, Emme and I began to take time to process all we knew. It was time for her to open the box where she had stored all her emotions since returning home. She was about to feel insecure and vulnerable, and it had to be done away from everyone so she would not be watched like she was the fish in a bowl. Ethan provided her a way to escape our friends by announcing to the dining room she was looking tired. I went to her and, against her protest, plucked her up and walked her to her room to speed along the process everyone leaving .

I could sense her mood shifting as she mentally opened her box, allowing her emotions to spill over.

"What am I supposed to do?" Emmeline asked, starting to cry. "Do we call Kramer? Do we have to go into hiding? What do you know that I don't? Does the whole Table want me dead? What will happen next?" Her voice becoming more and more high-pitched and erratic as she spoke.

"I don't know," I admitted, running my hand across my face and looking at her as she attempted to pace the covered porch.

I needed a cigarette and pulled one from the pack in my pocket that Emme hadn't seen yet. The situation just called for it tonight. The craving was too intense to ignore the smooth relief the nicotine provided.

"I don't have many options, do I?" she asked, pausing to give me a disgusted look. "I knew this day would come."

"We both did," I replied, taking a long drag of the cigarette. "We just have to do this like everything else. Look at it from the business perspective and find the best way to solve the problem. We know how to do that."

"I need you to stop smoking again." She curled her upper lip in mild disgust. She was the one who had convinced me to stop smoking the first time.

"Yeah, and I needed Thomas to never come near us again," I replied dryly. "I also need you to sit down."

Emmeline sighed heavily, complying with the request and finding a spot on the wooden swing. "I just want to obliterate him right now. The nerve of him to come here, to do this," she gestured to her stomach.

"Trust me, that feeling is mutual," I said, puffing a few more breaths on what she dubbed my cancer stick before stubbing the butt out in the potted plant.

"Now you make my plants smoke?" she complained as she positioned a decorative pillow behind her.

"Are you going to gripe at everything today?" I was still standing near the porch door but ready to pick up the pacing she had been doing earlier.

"Yes. I'm grumpy, sore, and just found out Thomas is the one who shot me. Speculation was one thing. To have evidence to prove it? Well, that is something else entirely."

"I know. That's a hard pill to swallow." I held her eyes until she couldn't look at me anymore.

Her next words were barely audible. "I know I'm the trader rat who left. But a deal was made. He's breaking the rules. The rules that I've followed to a tee."

"Yes, everyone gave up a lot for us to leave," I agreed.

"Yes, we did," she echoed. "We shouldn't have to be dealing with this. What game is he playing?"

"I want to know how The Table has been turned." Since I put the cigarette out, I had paced the length of the porch trying to reason out the whys. "Something has to have been changed, making him feel like he could do this."

"Always the rational mind," Emmeline said. She slowly stood back up, using her hand to support her healing belly. "I need to know what is going on. I think you should call him."

"Kramer is aware of the situation."

"Not him," she sighed, her exacerbation clear.

"Who?" I kept my back to her as I paused at the opposite side of the porch. If I played dumb, maybe she would drop this.

"Don't," she started. "I've let you pretend I didn't hear you talking to someone on the phone that day in the hospital. I don't care which one it was, but you need to reach back out."

My body tensed, "That's not how that works." I turned to see her eyeing me.

"And I'm not supposed to be in harm's way, yet here we are," Emmeline said firmly. She stood there, determined to push herself too far, too fast to be whole with one hand holding her abdomen in place, the other firmly on her hip. The familiar expression on her face was a command to do as she said. "Make the call," she demanded again.

She hadn't tried to order me around in years, and back then I would have jumped already. But that wasn't how we worked any longer. I had to run the advantages against the disadvantages of making that kind of call.

She read my expression and allowed herself to rest by sitting and stretching on the swing. She knew me well enough to realize I would have to find enough positive reasons to follow her demands. I could tell she hoped the numbers would add up for me to do so.

"Look, Joe," she started, throwing out my nickname as a way to butter me up. "I know it's not the best idea. I know calling whoever you do will be dangerous. We both know that. But if we are to have any tactical advantage over

Thomas, we have to know what's going on in their camp right now."

When I didn't answer, she kept going. "We have to get to the bottom of why he felt he could take such a bold action against me. We need to know how to move next. That call can give us that. You have been keeping some sort of relationship open if they had your number to begin with. Just do it for me," she pleaded.

I took a deep breath. "If I call and ask *anything*, it could put him in danger too."

"That's a risk we have to take," she countered. "Think about all the innocent people around us."

I could only nod my head in agreement. Even if I hated that, she was right.

She continued, "They could have done so much damage at that show. What if they show up here? Our PAs, employees, and friends are all here. We could be putting them in danger and they didn't sign up for that."

"Why do you always have to be right?" I sneered, pulling another cigarette out. If I had to call him, this cigarette was going to take the edge off. I was supposed to be waiting for him. He told me he'd have Jackson call with what he found out. But how could I deny her? She'd already been through so much.

For the last 15 years, Emmeline and I held a fear of what happened when the monsters hiding in the closet came out to play. We hadn't heard a peep from them. Jackson and I had the occasional check-in about generic things only. Nothing I could relay to Kramer or anything that implied danger was ever spoken. Emmeline hadn'tspoken to Him, her family, or any of our old friends since the day we were exiled. They lived their lives, we lived ours. All of us kept to the contract. We feared them but we had Kramer and our protection plan. We lived our lives. Now, Emmeline being shot meant there was no way the life and family we ended and walked away from would stay in the past. We could smile all we wanted, and make all the money we wanted. Sign all the publishing deals for artists. But no matter what, we both were scared of those monsters.

She dealt with it by micromanaging her life down to the second. As time passed, she started to believe maybe she would be fine; she could run her company and live her life. Her music helped her as well. I managed differently, attempting to keep us secure at all times; finding ways to deal with the fear was the best way to handle it. But unfortunately, this attempt on her life showed us that wasn't the case. Her past finally caught up to her present and now threatened our future. Now we had to work out what we were going to do about this.

"Here is my first issue," Emmeline started, bringing me out of my train of thought. "I'm not always right, but I am normally good with my intuition. I can't believe he's working on a family order. Maybe off a personal vendetta against us? Me?"

"Agreed." There was no way The Table would allow such a breach of contract.

"We can't take the risk with our friends."

"Agreed, again," I replied.

"The media and police are pressing the issues that can cause more problems," she added. "Kramer will need to intercede for us."

"If they uncover any of our past identities, it will bring too much scrutiny," I said, powering through my second cigarette.

"Our past is going to come up or we are going to have to go back to them," Emmeline said, her voice sounding small. "And we will face what we escaped."

"Neither of those options is one I want to happen," I replied, my voice soft and comforting.

"If Thomas is out for vengeance, maybe we should just let him have it," Emmeline whispered, her eyes no longer meeting mine.

"No," I said, my voice firm. "I can't have you speaking that way. Not now, not ever. I know you are worried, grumpy, and in pain, but that is no reason to doubt our choices."

"But," she tried to inject.

"No, no buts." I crossed the porch to her and squatted down to look her square in the eye. "What we chose was the best thing. This is just a setback. And if your gut is right and this is something between you and him? Well, we will settle it. Then life can go back to our kind of normal. If this is something more, then we will deal with that. You and I have each other's back; that is our deal."

Emmeline looked at me, and for the first time in years, I saw real tears in her eyes. "This is because I left. Because I didn't choose him. He wanted the Chair, and I refused him."

"I know. But we can't blame ourselves."

"What are you talking about? We have no one but ourselves to blame. The Fathers arranged a life we couldn't and didn't let happen. You know what we did."

"What we did was prevent the Fathers from having their way," I countered.

"That's why he had to stay behind, and that is why I was shot," she said, defeated.

"This is not the reason you were shot. He's a psychopath. That is why you were shot," I stated vehemently.

"No, I went to..." She paused and didn't say a name, but I immediately knew who she meant. "And ... well, I made him promise me he would not make life easy for the jackal. He did what I asked; and made sure his life was a living nightmare for the last 15 years. Last I heard, he had been committed to Silverwing Asylum for the Criminally Insane. I don't know when he was let out, but that has to be why I was shot. Revenge."

"You've hidden that all this time?"I asked, an edge to my voice. She never kept things from me. However, this was probably the last secret she had to share. I couldn't be angry. I also couldn't remember the last time I saw her genuinely cry. These were not the tears needed for a scene, but the type that comes from deep pain and guilt.

"It was my burden to bear. You had so many others to carry." She kept her voice low. "It was one thing I had with just him; our last bond."

Wrapping her in a hug, I whispered, "Then we will handle it."

"I need to confess something to you," I said after I let her go.

"Oh, God, what?" She asked, dread coating her features.

"You had a visitor after Shawn and Katy were banned from your hospital room."

"Who?" she asked wearily.

"Short-Stack."

"What?" Emmeline whimpered. "He was here?" Her face paled as her arms automatically wrapped around her small frame. Her face contorted as if she held in more tears she didn't want to fall. Her lips began to move as if to say something, but she either couldn't find the words or didn't know how to put a voice to them.

"Yes, I allowed him to sit with you," I said quietly.

"Oh, God," she breathed. "I thought I was dreaming."

"What?" I exclaimed. "You thought you dreamt what?"

"I just remember I was happy with him, that we were snuggled on a beach, maybe. It was just nice and warm. Are you telling me that wasn't a dream?"

I swallowed hard, "I mean, it might have been just a dream for you. But yes, he was here with you for a short time."

"How long?"

"An hour. I got a phone call, and then ... Well, I made him leave. He didn't fight me on it."

"Of course not," Emmeline said dryly. She turned and faced her yard, no longer fighting tears.

I didn't say a word as they came and stepped back into her bedroom. I went looking for a bottle of water and her pain pills. It was clear she was hurting, and the crying wouldn't help. As an afterthought, I found her a hanky and gathered a wet washcloth.

Emmeline sat on her swing and her tears flowed. I couldn't imagine the pain radiating from her stomach from her breathing and sobbing. I also couldn't imagine the heartache; it had been so long since Short-Stack had been in the same zip code as her, let alone the same room. She might have been unconscious, but still, her soul knew he was there. They were two halves of the same heart. It was clear the depth of her grief from the loss of him in her life.

As I stood watching her from the doorway, she began to shake from the sobs. I regretted saying anything. Our world was imploding in on itself; we had to figure out how to survive and now I had added this to her worries. I stepped back out and gathered her in my arms to comfort her.

"I'm sorry," she sobbed.

"For?" I asked, confused.

"Falling apart like this. I thought after all this time I had a better handle on it all." Her voice faded as she spoke.

"That is no reason to apologize." I paused for several beats, finding the correct phrase. "I'd be more worried if he still didn't affect you."

We exchanged a look, and I handed her the items I gathered in her room.

"I'm surprised no one has found us yet," she murmured.

"I put Ethan on guard," I laughed. Once she had pulled herself together, Emmeline slowly moved out of my embrace and then stepped into her room. Using a step stool to gingerly climb up on her four-poster bed, she snuggled down into her soft comforter.

"You need sleep," I said as I watched her settle in.

"Yes. This has been too much," she replied, confirming the obvious as a yawn escaped her. "I am so tired.I feel like I will pass out."

"I'd imagine that is hard for you," I deadpanned.

"It's not easy, that is for sure."

I took a deep breath, "I'm going to head back out there, and make sure the party is still going."

"That was no party. That was a wake," Emme grumbled. "All anyone has been doing is memorializing me. Like I died that day, everyone is so thankful I lived, but can't stop remembering things, as if I won't ever do anything again."

"I don't think they know how to handle this," I said, trying to soothe her frustrations.

"Well, neither do I," she snapped. Then sighed, letting go of whatever she was going to say. Emmeline snuggled deeper into her bed, "Don't wake me unless the house is on fire."

"Only a house fire?" I said rolling my eyes, "Sure thing, Emmes."

Leaving the room, I reminded Ethan to not let anyone disturb her, no matter what. She wanted to come home because she was tired of being emotionally strong. She needed to open her box and let go of all her pain so she could really rest.

Emmeline

After sleeping longer than I ever had at home, I woke up to see not only had all my friends left, but another day had passed, and it was dinner time.

"The house isn't on fire," Joe said as he spotted me. " But I'm glad you're up. We have to watch MIN tonight," as I walked into the living room.

I rolled my eyes, "Okay, why?" I went straight for the couch, my body was achy.

"Well, the promos promised revealing information about the mystery of who shot you," he replied nonchalantly.

"Joy," I said, rolling my eyes. Sleep had done wonders for me and my headspace, but everything still felt wrong. Life was going to be a battle for a while.

Glancing at the clock I saw I had a couple hours until the broadcast. "Lydia check in today?" I asked.

"Just a few texts," he answered casually. "Nothing worth mentioning."

"Did you let it get weird while I was unconscious?"

"We had a few moments, both good and bad," he admitted easily. "She is still the love of my life. Not that it matters anymore."

"Joseph, I'm sorry," I said hoping he could hear the heartbreak in my voice for him. More than anything, I wanted him to be happy and content with his love life.

"Yeah, I know," he said softly. "I can love her and protect her from afar. It sucks. But it's for the best."

A commercial for MIN caught our attention, distracting us from romantic woes.

"Tonight, we are looking into the shooting of Emmeline Jones with special guest Terri Goodman. You don't want to miss what we uncovered. We have the answers you have been waiting for," the voiceover promised. A series of photos of me from all eras of my career passed across the screen, finishing with a graphic of the time and the streaming channel to watch the live broadcast.

"Did you make the call?" I asked suddenly, now more than curious about what Alyson Summers and stupid entertainment news show could know.

"No," he stated. "And before you get mad, let me tell you why," he added quickly.

I cocked my eyebrow but allowed him to continue.

"Short-Stack and I talked before he left."

My heart lurched at the mention of him but I attempted to keep my face unreadable.

"Summary—he didn't allow this, he's looking into it and James will contact me when he knows anything."

I turned back to the TV as an advertisement for a fast food chain and their new double-decker burger with a special sauce played. "I'm hungry," I mumbled.

"Okay," he said dryly, immediately getting up to tend to my needs.

"I knew he hadn't allowed it," I whispered to myself, feeling the relief of knowing Short-Stack was still on my side. "Thomas either went rogue, or he has a different family backing him," I said louder so Joe would hear me. "No matter what, Thomas shot me. He failed dramatically or did exactly what he wanted, which was to destroy my life."

A plate appeared in front of me and I dug into the pasta concoction that smelt heavenly.

"Tomorrow I intend to reach out to Kramer," Joe said with a frustrated look. "Then contact all the lawyers to get a game plan but together."

"We need to tell Lydia something," I added.

"Oh, I know," he snorted.

"Do you want to handle that?" I asked, taking another bite, wondering what exactly I had missed.

"Nope, we'll do that together," he rolled his eyes, a sentence dying on his lips.

"Gotcha, we'll be on the same page."

"Let me fill you in on all that happened while you were taking your morphine nap," he pivoted the conversation as he returned to his seat.

"Do you mean while you were keeping me heavily sedated?"

"To-ma-to, ta-ma-toe." Joe shrugged his shoulders. He'd never apologize for something he thought was for my benefit.

He went into great detail about all the events from the moment he saw me misstep on stage until I told him to bring me home. I missed a lot when I was in my dreamscapes. It was a good thing the TV was already on and tuned to the right streaming channel to catch the opening credits of MIN because after the story he weaved, I would have been okay just shutting down for a bit.

"One week after the shooting of pop star Emmeline Jones, there are still many questions about who the shooter was and why the attempt was made on her life," Alyson Summers started her broadcast. She had a graphic in the lower left corner of the screen with the streaming count of viewers on it. I watched as it was rising quickly.

The reporter stood in front of her classic backdrop, looking very business-like. In drastic contrast, I was propped up on the couch in my sweats while Joseph was on the opposite couch with a laptop and some rice mixture he kept in the fridge for a snack.

"Police investigations have been halted due to lack of leads and cold trails. While there is a photograph of the suspect, no databases have been able to determine who it was. Ms. Jones and her team have been cooperating with the police, but even she could not identify this suspect."

Alyson looked dramatically into a camera on her left and then continued, "But all evidence points to the fact this was a personal assault on Ms. Jones, leaving all of us to question who would want to harm Emmeline Jones?"

"When we return, special guest, Ms. Terri Goodman, shares details on why this might have happened and what Emmeline Jones didn't do to prevent this."

The gossip news show took a commercial break, and Joseph shut his computer. I sat up a bit straighter.

"What can they know?" Joseph asked. "They can't know more than me, than us?"

"Your guess is as good as mine," I sighed.

"I can already tell I don't like this," he gruffed. "But whatever she has, it doesn't matter. It's for ratings."

When the show came back on, Alyson and Terri sat opposite each other at a desk. They both had note cards in hand, and the show no longer looked like a trashy gossip program but more like a news program or special segment.

"Oh, this is so bad," I gasped. "Please welcome to the show, Terri Goodman, feature writer at the *Hollywood Herald*, the national Phoenix Merit Winner magazine."

"Thank you for having me," Terri said. Her demeanor was much like it was on the day of the personal interview with me almost two years ago–all business.

"We've both been following Ms. Jones's career for several years now in a professional capacity."

"Yes, we have," Terri agreed with a smile.

"What is one thing about her you've always noticed?" Alyson asked.

"That she's very guarded," Terri jumped in immediately. "She announced her world tour with me and we discussed upcoming projects. And while she was open to speak about her company and projects, she refused to discuss anything personal. It was obvious in my interview that she kept a very close track on how she would speak of anything outside of her work."

"I've always thought that too," Alyson agreed. "We know nothing about her on a personal level."

Terri nodded and continued, "Yes, while we have seen her in many alleged romances she has never acknowledged anything other than business. More curious is her interactions with Joseph MacDonald. They cleave to their business titles, denying anything between the two of them, but all their body language screams much more."

"Exactly. When MIN obtained this photograph," Alyson paused as a photo of me at 17, wrapped in the arms of an 18-year-old Joseph at the ribbon cutting ceremony of our company popped on the screen. "They denied all claims they were a couple."

"That is one example," Terri added. "During our time together, I wanted her to open up about who she was as a person, outside of the circus, but she refused. Which only left me with more questions."

"Can you elaborate more on your interview with the announcement?"

"She was very evasive in regards to her background. Her body language was guarded," Terri described. "At first I believed it was because of personal control issues but after many months of investigating the subject, it has led me to another conclusion altogether."

"And what conclusion was that, Terri??" Alyson pressed.

"Well, Alyson, that led me to ask, 'Who is Emmeline Jones?'"

"When we return, we will find out what Terri has uncovered and possibly answer that very question," Alyson dropped the line smoothly before the broadcast went to another commercial break.

My heart sank; this interview was just the thing that could wreck everything for me. It was essential to keep my past where it belonged—behind me. No one needed to ask too many questions because I wasn't sure how easy it would be to find my former truths. This was why I had made so many boundaries and kept so many rules.

Joe quickly disappeared through the kitchen. I heard the patio door open and knew he was lighting another cigarette. I would have to get him those stupid patches to help him quit again.

I was left to my dark thoughts during the break and breathed out as Joseph entered just as the show came back. I wanted to pace but settled for pressing my fingers into my collarbone to settle my breathing.

"Welcome back to our special edition on Emmeline Jones," Alyson greeted her viewers. She rehashed who her guest was and then dived right back in with Terri, asking her what she had uncovered.

Joe sat on the coffee table, his posture rigid.

"I decided to go to the very beginning," Terri recalled. She easily sat at the desk, comfortable speaking to Alyson and the camera, telling her tale.

"Everything about her company is well documented. But when I looked deeper into the start of Lillian James Productions I found a curious fact. All purchases were cash."

"Meaning?" Alyson prompted.

"Meaning that two teenagers just had enough capital to fund their fantasy careers?"

"That seems highly unlikely," Alyson replied in a knowing tone.

"Exactly, so where did the money come from? That in combination with the answer Emmeline gave when I asked about her education, raised more questions. She would never say a specific degree she had earned or institution she went to."

"So you couldn't find her transcripts from her college?"

"No, Alyson, I couldn't find anything about Emmeline's past, her childhood, or her education. Nothing. I immediately ran into a roadblock with my search," Terri started. "Using every legal resource available to me, I've been unable to find a birth certificate, school records, medical information, or anything else for Emmeline Jones. No trace of anything."

Alyson looked as if she was hearing this for the first time as she asked, her acting as bad as her reporting "What do you believe this means?"

"It means," Terri leaned toward the camera, "Emmeline Jones does not exist."

"Well, clearly she does. We have followed her since her break-out role in *On Point* and her self-titled, debut album," Alyson deadpanned.

"That is true. But Emmeline Jones is a created identity. Just another character to act out for all of us."

"Why would she deceive everyone in such a manner?"

"That is what I'll answer in my long-awaited article, hitting newsstands this Friday," Terri dropped strategically.

"Come on, isn't there anything else you can tell us?" Alyson probed.

Terri nodded with a sly grin on her face, "This shooting incident was preventable."

"How so?" Alyson looked aghast—all she needed was pearls to clutch.

"Emmeline might not be cooperating with the police as much as her camp claims she is. Along with lying about who she is, I believe there is a reason she is not being completely truthful with authorities. My whole theory will be explained in the piece featured in the *Hollywood Herald*. All I can say is Emmeline Jones isn't who she tries so hard to be."

With that, Alyson turned to the camera, "So, who is Emmeline Jones? And what is she hiding?" And with that, Alyson ended her program, a promotion for her next episode running as the credits ran across the screen.

"This is a complete and utter disaster," I cried out, leaping from my seat. The pain shot through my body, but I was too hyper-aware of the secrets that could be released on newsstands Friday.

"Please sit back down," Joseph demanded.

"Who is Emmeline Jones? And what is she hiding? You want to tell me how this isn't the end of the world?" I repeated as I continued to pace. This was just the PR nightmare I was terrified of.

"If you do not sit down," Joe's voice warned, his tone stern.

As I was pacing, my breathing hitched and became erratic.

"You are giving yourself a panic attack," Joe continued. "Please just sit down."

"But did you hear her?" I gestured to the TV.

"I did." He stood up and blocked my path, "Please sit down." He rubbed his hands down my arms soothing me for a few moments before holding both my hands.

"Joseph," I whispered his name like it was my lifeline. I thought I had mentally prepared for the day when the rug was swept out from under us.

He led me back to the couch and pulled me into his lap. "Look, this is a terrible, horrible reality. But you and I have each others back. We will figure this out and deal with it."

I wanted the world to pause, just for a moment, when I felt secure. But it quickly became impossible to ignore the buzzing of our phones on the coffee table.

Joe reached over and grabbed his, "Hello," he answered, shifting me to keep me in his arms and allowing us both space. He then put the phone on speaker and I heard a familiar, stern voice come through.

"What do I need to know?" Lydia directly stated, stress coating her voice.

"Are you already in the office?" Joseph asked knowingly.

"I'm headed there right now," she snarled. "I started heading in after I saw the piece."

"I'll meet you there in a bit. Right now, just ignore anything and everything. We'll put together a statement and get a handle on this."

"How bad is the reaction?" I interjected, needing to know just what this meant for my public figure.

"Right now, I only see support coming in from your fan base," she said softly. Then her tone flooded with accusation as she continued, "But whatever you are hiding from me, whatever Terri Goodman knows? Well, it better be worth it."

I didn't like what she said or how she said it, but I knew the woman spoke the truth. It would be a coin toss if the fans would rally around me or cancel me once that article came out. I looked at Joe, who was contemplating the next move.

While Terri hadn't said who or what was in my past, the implication of secrets was there and that could end anyone's career.

"Lydia, just go to the office and wait for me and Ms. Jones," Joe ordered.

"Will do boss," she replied to the curtness in his voice.

During the drive to the office, Joe and I didn't speak. He knew I needed the time to put myself together. I might be a robot when it came to work, but when it came to everything in my past—my story and secrets—it was still raw. I also knew Joe would need to pull his thoughts together so he would have the right approach with Lydia. Especially after he had been so harsh with her in the thick of my hospital stay.

As we arrived at the office and filed into the elevator, I put on my Emmeline mask and prepared to face the first hurdle.

What's next for Emmeline?

Find out in:

The Education of Emmeline Jones

By MM Hurley

Coming Soon

Acknowledgements

Any book is a labor of love and sacrifice, this is no different. The first thing I have to do is acknowledge the love and sacrifices that my friends and family have made. And I wouldn't be here today if I didn't recognize that. This may be my idea but I wouldn't have to get it to this place, a book in someone else's hands with the love and support of my amazing family and friends. There are so many that along the way have helped or offered support or excitement about what I was trying to do. The people listed here are just the people who helped. I know I wouldn't be even doing this if I didn't have the gift of writing. It's my wholehearted belief I was given this gift at a young age because the Lord knew my speaking ability would be low. I jumble up my words, lose my train of thought, and am not a conversationalist. I have to thank my Heavenly Father for that gift.

First, I have to thank my dear amazing husband. Hubby, you and I married at a young age and many believed that it would never last. But here we are 18+ years later with four beautiful children. You have never once told me to give up this writing thing. You supported me while I finished college, pursuing my journalism degree. You helped me balance our crazy life and still take the time to work as much as I could here and there on my stories. You listen to me go on my rabbit hole word vomit tirades about this and that. You have been an incredible husband all these years. Thank you for wanting this for me. Thank you for dealing with all my crazy and all that I am to get me to this point of my dream. Even if this flops in the biggest of big ways; thank you for your unwavering love and devotion and support of my dreams.

Now, my dear sister. Becky Jones, I thank you so much for all that you are to me: my first best friend, my cheerleader, my pain in the butt, and everything in between. I thank you for every moment you've stopped to help me. You're reading and feedback. Your knowledge of grammar and the gentle way you point out my flaws with ways to fix them. The photoshoot for the perfect jacket photo and all the help you have given me over the years with not only this book but all my writing. Thanks sissy.

Next, my editor, best friend, and all-around cheerleader, Trista Lutgring. TJ, you have been one of my longest friends, and when I approached you about tackling this with me, you didn't hesitate. You were ready to take it on. I'm sure you have repeatedly rolled your eyes at me as we have gone through the editing process. And I'm thoroughly aware that I've probably bugged you a million more times than I should have. But the time and energy you put into my story has been nothing short of charity work. You have been helpful, supportive, kind, and generous. With working a full-time job and having a life of your own, you still took the time to work countless hours on making this story blossom into something more than a random idea of a desperate writer who just wanted to make it work. Thank you friend for being there for me and being the one I could trust to go down this road with.

Another friend I have to mention and thank is my first reader, Christy Hensley. You have been nothing but my biggest cheerleader for the longest time. Each time I have shared anything with you; you have given me the best feedback. You have watched me work, sitting silently alongside me while I had to get something down before losing it. You have just always been the one who has told me I can do this, that my work is meaningful, and that others will like it too. I can't thank you enough for the love you have given me. I appreciate you so much.

Another random person that I want to thank, is George Herrod. Mr. Herrod is an instructor at my kid's karate school. He pours himself into teaching the kiddos at that school about the movements and good moral traits. He's talked to them about empathy, kindness, and being good people. And while I've sat for countless hours in the karate school, watching my kids grow, I was also taking the hour here and there to write, edit, read, and just try to do something with my book., This man took the time to cheer me on, being a ray of sunshine, and asking questions about what I was doing and writing. He didn't owe me anything, but he supported me in a way that I needed. Generally, just taking the time to be interested. I can't express how much I appreciate that. So, thank you Mr. Herrod not only for what you have done with my kiddos, but for the support you showed to me.

I have to thank Jeana Henry for answering all my hypothetical medical questions. Letting me know those spots where I have no medical knowledge didn't sound as incredibly stupid as I am sure they do. And I still cross my heart that this is all hypothetical and not actual personal medical history I'm asking you about. Also thank you for buying me a milkshake on one of the worst days of my life.

Next, I have to thank Valerie Gore. Without your support and generosity, I would have never been able to publish this. I can't say enough thanks to you for your contributions to this book and future books. I will never forget how you took a worry off my plate and just made it perfect. As an educator for years, you have impacted so many students, but as a friend you have not only blessed me but supported my dream in a way I can never repay.

Finally, I have to thank my Mom and Dad. It's been a long time since I've been under your roof, with you two as my guardians; however, you have still been taking care of me long since the requirement for you to do so expired. As a child, you taught me that my word was my word; and not to break it. I gave you both my word I'd finish school when I left it to marry and have my oldest child. And we know that I did. But I also gave you my word that I'd do my best at this whole life thing, and this is me–doing my best to follow my dreams. The life I planned at 16 didn't pan out quite the way I thought it should, but with you both supporting me in all my crazy, here I am at nearly 40 doing the thing that scares me, keeping my word and publishing this book. I thank you both for the name Hurley, for the lessons, the joy, and the love you have given me all my life.

OTHER WORKS AVAILABLE:

Journals:

- Class Notes
- Sermon Scriptures
- Weekly Journals
- Daily Journals

With more options coming soon.

MM HURLEY

- WKU Grad
- Mom of Four
- Chaos Coordinator
- Volunteer Extraordinaire
- Aspiring Author

For more info:
mmhurley.com